Almost
AGATHA
CHRISTIE

Cenarth Fox

Almost Agatha Christie

First published in 2020 by Fox Plays
www.cenfoxbooks.com
www.foxplays.com

ISBN 978 0 949175 45 8

Cover design by Oliviaprodesign

Lady Mallowan

She was Agatha Miller, Agatha Christie, Agatha Mallowan, Mary
Westmacott and Dame Agatha. She is the Queen of Crime.
Her writing output is Guinness Book of Records material.
After the Bard, she's the most popular author.
At first, publishers rejected her manuscripts.
Where are those publishers today?

In Agatha Christie's novel, *The Body in the Library*, one reads the
name Dorothy Sayers.

'Very few of us are what we seem.'
'The best time to plan a book is while you're doing the dishes.'
Agatha Christie 1890—1976

The Changing Calendar

A few dates in this novel have been given a wee shove.
In some quarters it's known as artistic licence.

For
The cast and crew of theatre companies
which have staged the comedy *Agatha Crispie*

Photos, reviews and preview script of *Agatha Crispie* at
www.foxplays/two-actplays.com

Chapter 1

AGATHA DID AS SHE WAS TOLD. It was the story of her life. Being an only child, her parents were royalty, god-like and what they decreed, she obeyed. Queen Victoria ruled the Empire, and Fred and Margaret Taylor ruled the detached bungalow in Teddington with a south facing garden. It was close to schools and public transport. As a student, Agatha excelled at being average where her favourite subject was reading. She lived, explored and escaped through books.

'You'll damage your eyes, Agatha,' her mother would say as the 12 year old curled up with yet another book, her second that afternoon.

But it wasn't just reading which fascinated Agatha. She felt the urge to write. Poetry at first, the kind of thing you bury beneath your pyjamas in the bottom drawer and never show to anyone. But it was a start, and the urge to put pencil to paper persisted.

Her father, Fred, was a misfit. One could be cruel and say he travelled in ladies' underwear when in fact he sold dress materials, dress-making patterns and whatever else he could cram into his battered suitcase. Being a Londoner, he could do his rounds, be home for tea, and sleep in his own bed every night. Alas, what little money he made slipped easily through his fingers.

Margaret, the homemaker, maintained an anti-dust policy inside the bungalow with a kitchen floor you could use as a dining-table. She and Fred had a marriage where the couple could well be taken for brother and sister. Agatha rarely saw her parents so much as touch one another let alone share a kiss or a hug. The closest they came to intimacy was when passing crockery as they shared washing-up duties. Years later, Agatha wondered how she was ever conceived.

Her parents married later in life and, without siblings, Agatha at times felt she was living in a retirement home. When Queen Victoria finally relinquished the throne, Fred relinquished his. He gave up work and soon thereafter gave up breathing. He died in his sleep and enjoyed the highest quality cheap funeral.

'Well, Agatha,' said Margaret to her now twenty year old daughter, 'you, my girl will have to find a proper job.'

'Yes, Mother.'

'Your father was useless with money but fortunately my father made him take out a life insurance policy on the mortgage so at least we have a debt-free roof over our heads.'

'Yes, Mother.'

'And when I shuffle off this mortal coil, all this will be yours. Of course, in the meantime, you could find yourself a husband but with your head continually buried in a book, and your dream of being a famous writer a pathetic pipedream, I think marriage for you, young lady, is a non-starter.'

'Yes Mother.'

'And now your great aunts and their duplicitous daughters have finally settled their pointless disagreement over your grandmother's will, Mummy's maid Pimms will be coming to live with us. You remember Pimms?'

Agatha did but not fondly. When staying with her grandmother, six year old Agatha had to sit still while the maid read her a story. Agatha couldn't understand the unusual smell—or was it smells?—emanating from the maid, or her mispronunciation of words even the young Agatha knew to be wrong. She dared not correct the whiffy dyslexic.

'I'm pleased you will have the company, Mummy,' said Agatha.

'Why?' asked Margaret, 'are you thinking of leaving?'

Actually Agatha had considered flying the nest, quietly planning such a move, but for now she kept the idea under wraps. '*Extra* company, I mean,' replied Agatha. 'And I will begin looking for a paying job now Daddy has left us.'

'Left us to fend for ourselves you mean.'

'Yes Mother.'

'Well, what can you do? What would like to do? And don't say you want to be a writer.'

'I can continue to volunteer, Mother. The churches and hospitals are always looking for people to help.'

'I thought you said a paying job. How much money will volunteering bring into the house? Well?'

'I will gain valuable life experiences, Mother, and might meet someone who can recommend me for a possible paying job.'

This was reasonable logic leaving Mother stumped for something critical to say—for once. The next morning Agatha walked to the vicarage of her local church to be welcomed by the vicar's housekeeper.

'You've just missed him, Miss Taylor. Can I tell him you called?'

'Yes please, Mrs Trembath.'

'How is your mother, dear? And how are you? We're all thinking about you and praying for you and your dear mother.'

'We're both as well as can be expected, thank you. I wanted to ask the vicar about doing more volunteer work.'

'Good for you, Miss. You keep busy. I'll tell the Reverend Frawley.'

And so Agatha began working as a volunteer with the Church Missionary Society. She needed to join the work force for personal development and paid employment reasons, but she needed to escape the house for as long as possible because her grandmother's long-serving maid, Pimms—nobody was sure of her real name or in fact if that was her name—moved in as her mother's companion. She could hardly be her mother's maid in a small two and a half bedroom bungalow in suburban Teddington. Pimms won the boot room, the bedroom where you had to step outside to change your mind.

Agatha's grandmother, Ottilie, hired Pimms last century when both women were young. Mind you, it was hard to imagine Pimms ever being youthful. Part of Ottilie's will required Pimms to be taken in by Ottilie's eldest daughter, Margaret Taylor of Teddington.

Welcome Pimms.

Agatha's theory about meeting someone when volunteering in the hope of finding paid employment paid off. When folding linen parcels with a kind woman from Hampton Hill, Mrs Horton told Agatha about her daughter getting married, and leaving her job as a pharmacy assistant at St Thomas' Hospital in London.

Being a brick, Mrs Horton wrote Agatha a lovely reference, as did the head of the CMS, as well as Agatha's vicar. She got the job.

Margaret was shocked. 'You've found a job?'

'Yes Mother.'

'A proper job?'

'Yes, Mother.'

'A paying job?'

'Yes Mother.'

'In London?'

'Yes Mother.'

'I think the girl's pretty clever,' said Pimms which silenced Mother and made Agatha smile. She went to her room, terribly excited, took out her exercise book number 14 and wrote a poem about happiness. Once finished, she placed it back under the winter nighties in her bottom drawer, and wrote a letter to her best friend Beatrice "Bea" Hopkiss. They were as thick as thieves and had been ever since meeting on holiday in Bognor Regis years ago.

"I've got a job, Bea, I've got a job!"

Not being able to see one another often, if at all, the young women became avid letter writers and kept the Royal Mail in business.

> *Dear Aggie*
> *Congratulations, my darling. Who's a clever*
> *girl then? Write and tell me all about being*
> *an assistant in a pharmacy. And now you're*
> *in a hospital, you might meet a dashing*
> *doctor or two. Good luck with those gents.*
> *You won't be surprised to hear I'm still stuck*
> *with you know who.*
> *Love*
> *Bea*

Working at the pharmacy in St Thomas' Hospital was hectic with all sorts of concoctions being made up for all sorts of patients. Agatha was the assistant to the assistant, a young woman with a lust for life. Clara Higginbotham's red hair matched her personality. She was the perfect work colleague for Agatha, drawing her out of her shell and pushing her to join in the game of life.

Mother looked askance as her daughter wore more makeup and bought herself a hat she deemed most inappropriate.

'It's what all the young ladies are wearing, Mother.'

'Your father would never have sold such a hat.'

'I rather like it,' said Pimms which put Mother in a spin. Without trying, the young Agatha and the much older Pimms were becoming, well, a sort of a team, a mutual admiration society. Mother was not pleased and entertained certain thoughts.

How can I get rid of this maid? Whose side is she on, anyway?

But make-up and clothes were not the only changes in Agatha's life. Romance won her heart. Clara knew a girl who had a friend who knew a social butterfly who knew about a dance next Saturday. Clara, temporarily without a beau, simply had to go and asked Agatha to join her.

Well, that caused a scene at Avenue Road, Teddington in sleepy Middlesex. 'Don't be ridiculous, Agatha. It's out of the question. Your father wouldn't even dream of letting you go out on your own.'

'But I won't be on my own, Mother. I'm to go with my work colleague, Miss Higginbotham.'

'And where is this so-called dance? And who will be there?'

'It's a social function for Royal Navy officers and crew from the *HMS Gloucester*, Mother. Last year, Prince Edward, the Prince of Wales attended this same function.'

Good call, Aggie. Royalty proved hard to argue against for lower middle-class Margaret. She struggled to find a reason for her daughter to remain at home, and away from men in general and sailors in particular. She wasn't helped by the wretched maid who chose to sing to *la* a song from *HMS Pinafore*.

'Well how will you get home?' demanded Mother.

'Clara's brother will meet us after the dance, and accompany us to and on the train.'

'And how will you travel from Teddington Station? It must be at least half a mile to our place.' To try and win the argument, Mother exaggerated wildly; in truth it was just over a furlong to the station.

Ah, at last; Mother found the question to foil the fun. Clara and her brother would remain on the train to their stop at Hampton Wick leaving Agatha to walk the 245 yards to her home. Not acceptable.

Before she could try and assure her mother it would be all right, the whiffy dyslexic jumped in.

'I'll meet Miss Agatha at the station and walk her home, Madam.'

Mother was stymied again. She couldn't refuse, and what became interesting was the relationship switch. Pimms and the daughter grew closer while the maid and the mother drifted apart.

Whether Margaret's flippant remark about Agatha spending her life reading and thus never finding a husband triggered romantic thoughts in Agatha's head, we can't be sure. But the invitation to the dance kick-started a new interest for Agatha—sex.

Reading and writing were not her only hobbies or skills as she soon fell in love with dancing. She reveled in it and it showed. It was a Royal Navy dance and sailors and shore crew soon saw what a lively lass Miss Agatha Taylor from Teddington was, and boy, could that gal fox-trot! She had her pick of seafarers. Of all the "boys" she danced with, one caught her eye and then her heart. Harry Crispie was a Sub-Lieutenant in Britain's fleet and he looked spiffing in uniform.

No sooner had Mother scoffed at her daughter's lack of marital prospects, Agatha met Sub-Lieutenant Harry Crispie and love was in the air. First cab off the rank and Agatha struck gold. When Agatha brought Harry home to meet Mother and the maid, Margaret went all coy and Pimms all chirpy. Margaret was more shocked than excited. Her little girl had grown up. A wee while later, when Harry proposed and Agatha accepted, Margaret began blaming her late husband.

'Where is Fred when I need him? I'll need a new dress and hat and shoes; oh a complete new outfit. The mother of the bride is the most important person at the wedding.' Pimms and Agatha sighed.

Pimms, who had spent years looking after Agatha's grandmother muttered, 'Like mother, like daughter.'

> *Dear Bea*
> *I'm engaged! The sailor I told you about,*
> *Harry Crispie, the one with the blue eyes and*
> *the fabulous dancing feet, has proposed and*
> *I've accepted. Can you believe it? So we need*
> *to meet, girl. The bridesmaid and the bride*
> *have a lot to talk about.*
> *Love*
> *Aggie*

Service personnel romances were tricky and especially for naval lads. With hormones on song, and orders to embark for foreign shores often in the air, pressure mounted. When are you free, sailor? When do you sail away and for how long?

The couple found a free fortnight and a small wedding was deemed best, particularly as the bride's family, such as it was, lacked the funds for anything beyond modest.

With no father, uncle or brother to give away the bride, Agatha's best friend suggested her father, Flanders, as the stand-in escort for the bride. Bea Hopkiss donned her bridesmaid's outfit and Mr Hopkiss did a splendid job walking down the aisle with Agatha, the beaming bride on his arm. Mother and Maid shed a tear. As for Pimms, it was a single tear in keeping with her response when offered a Pimms. Then she was wont to say, 'just the one'.

The wedding service in St Mary's, Teddington was basic, the reception, upstairs at the local public house was cramped, and the honeymoon in the Lake District was short and sensuous. Agatha's heart filled with enough love to see her through the long months when Harry was away at sea. Miss Agatha Taylor, now Mrs Harry Crispie, moved into a small flat near hubby's naval base and began volunteer work at the local hospital.

Harry was at sea so Bea came to stay and the two friends got on like a wooden house on fire. Their laughter became infectious but

7

disappeared when Bea hopped out of bed one night having heard her friend throwing up in the bathroom.

Bea said, 'Knock, knock,' as she opened the door to find her friend on her knees vomiting into the lavatory.

'I'm okay,' protested Agatha. 'I should never have eaten the seafood,' as another serve of last night's fish supper launched itself from Agatha and into the pan.

Eventually they made it to the kitchen where Bea fussed making weak black tea. Spinster, virginal Bea broached the subject. 'You know what this means, Agatha Crispie,' she said. 'You, my girl, are in the pudding club.'

Agatha knew but was nervous. This was a whole new experience for her and all she could think of was her husband. 'How can I tell Harry?' Bea was more businesslike.

'Forget Harry for now. You need to get your confinement sorted. We'll go to the hospital first thing in the morning. If you are with child, my darling, you may need to retire from volunteering.'

'But if I *am* pregnant, how can I tell Harry?' She cried and worried about this new experience; one she didn't want to face on her own.

Bea hugged her friend. 'I'm here, Aggie. And I'll stay for as long as you need me.'

Best friends, they both had a good cry.

The news was as expected. Agatha was pregnant, and Harry hard to contact. When the news reached Teddington, Margaret and Pimms both needed a strong drink.

'I'm going to be a grandmother,' gasped Margaret. 'What do grandmothers wear? I need Fred to help with my wardrobe.'

'Queen Victoria wore black, Madam,' said Pimms trying to be helpful. 'I've always believed the fewer outfits one has the better, and I'm a great believer in black being ideal for all occasions; it hides the stains an' all.'

Margaret might have understood the practical nature of Pimms' comment had Margaret not been struggling to cope with the news from her daughter.

'I hope it's a boy,' she said, 'and they call him Fred.'

'And what if it's a girl, Madam?' asked Pimms.

'What?'

'What should they call the child if it's a girl?'

'Oh I'm sure it'll be a boy. I've had a vision.'

Pimms looked at her current employer. Ottilie had been strange and it appeared her daughter Margaret displayed similar aspects of her Mummy's whacky nature. *Meet Mystic Meg* thought Pimms.

Weeks went by and Agatha's abdomen began to swell. Bea stayed as long as she dared but eventually left because, as full-time carer of her ailing mother, she headed home to Suffolk to resume nursing duties.

Agatha moved back home to Teddington for family support but, after a difficult few days, found Mother and Maid to be more of a nuisance than a nurse, and so returned to her flat in Portsmouth.

Harry received the news he was to be a father at about the time the tragedy occurred. Agatha was alone, which only compounded her misery. She was five months pregnant when, without warning, she miscarried. The shock left her numb. Living alone left her speechless. She wanted to cry and cry out but could do neither. She heard a neighbour and yelled. Explaining her situation was too difficult other than to say an ambulance was required.

24 hours after Harry heard of his impending fatherhood, his commanding officer had him sit down for another news bulletin. No toasting took place when the sub-lieutenant returned to quarters.

As soon as she heard the news, Bea raced to Agatha and stayed until Harry eventually made it home. When he did, the household had moved from joyful anticipation to silent woe. The bleak mood grew bleaker. Had the loss of the unborn child damaged the marriage? What was happening? Domestic chores became boring, hated tasks. Conversations between Harry and Agatha proved difficult.

Of course he couldn't blame her and felt responsible not being on hand when help was needed. Agatha's body was poorly and Harry quickly sensed any intimacy at this time was not a consideration. His leave was only for a week and soon he was away.

I must go down to the seas again, to the lonely sea and the sky.

He left and afterwards, Agatha returned to her work as a volunteer at the local hospital. Life for the living goes on. Counselling for the grieving Agatha was thin on the ground.

Darling Bea
I wish I had good news, glad news and happy
news. Alas no, I am alone and miserable.
Harry has been and gone and we parted
without love and barely a kiss. I will continue
to write to him and hope and pray. If you can
get away, you know where I am.
Love
Aggie

There were many letters between Bea and Agatha and occasional visits up to London to see Mother and Maid. Rather than lift her daughter's spirits, Margaret depressed everyone, her health too becoming an issue.

With Harry still at sea, Agatha's greatest consolation was her reading and writing. She borrowed from the local library and her writing itch constantly needed scratching. She read mysteries and moved her writing from poetry to prose and thus to short stories. She remembered advice she heard when a woman, who had written several mystery novels, spoke at a meeting of the WI.

'Write about what you know,' she said. 'Use the events and experiences in your life as inspiration for your writing.'

Agatha's writing did flourish although the routine of burying manuscripts beneath her bloomers in the chest of drawers continued.

A letter arrived from Harry. He rarely replied to the many letters she sent to him. It was brief—he had none of his wife's literary expertise—and the last line caused Agatha to feel ill. "There is something we need to discuss, Agatha." That night she couldn't sleep.

In the past she would go to the quayside with the other wives and families ready to greet her sailor when he came ashore. This time, something warned her off such a move. If she was going to be hurt, she wanted it to be private, and so remained at home.

When he appeared, his face spoke volumes. His words were bullets. At least he didn't waste time or try sugar-coating the bitter pill. He didn't love Agatha any more. He had met someone else. The best thing for both of them would be a clean break. Divorce was more common today. There were no children involved. Goodness! Where did all that come from?

Harry saw no point in discussing the situation. He didn't want a soft landing. His mind was made up, and Agatha had pain and shock to deal with in spades. For her, the evening was the first of many sleepless nights with plenty of wet pillows.

Harry slept in the spare room and didn't lose a wink of sleep. He sailed away from Agatha and, in Edwardian times in English society, the dreaded appendage, divorcee, would soon become attached to Mrs Agatha Crispie.

She ached all over. Who wouldn't? She loved Harry and couldn't understand why he left her sans warning. She soon discovered the truth. He'd found a floozy. Every nice girl loves a sailor.

Agatha's physical pain came from her mental anguish. She didn't want to eat, and spent hours fretting and self-loathing. She was a mess. Good for weight loss, not that Agatha needed it.

Amidst the pain and shock, the one line from Harry which stayed with Agatha for an age was, "I want you to have your freedom".

Was this a typical cheating husband's tactic? I'm ending our relationship for my reasons. I'm the cheating so-and-so, the cad, but to show I'm not all beastly, I'll be generous. I'll do the right thing here and you're the one being rewarded. Here's my gift. "I want you to have your freedom". What a line. What a cop out. What a rat.

The salt in the wound was not that Harry had fallen for a girl in every port; no, just the one. But not Gibraltar, Genoa or Gdansk; in fact she was a local lass from Portsmouth. That hurt. Doubly so when Agatha later discovered Harry's new beau was an old beau, an old flame he courted long before he met Miss Taylor.

Once Bea got the news, she urged her friend to make the name change. Her letters were full of love but included blunt advice.

Darling Aggie
I think you should go back to being Miss
Taylor. You'll be asked about your husband if
you remain Mrs Crispie. Forget him and be
your gorgeous, wonderful self again.
Love
Bea

Dearest Bea
I like the name Crispie. I've decided to write
under that name and I don't care about my
marital status. If people choose to look down
on me then that's their problem, not mine.
Love
Aggie

Bea sighed as she read Agatha's letter. She loved her friend and admired her strength in trying to make her way in life as a divorcee.

Agatha moved back to Teddington where her depression mixed with her mother's onset of early stage dementia, and Pimms' melancholy at having become a nursemaid to her former employer's now bedridden daughter. Three women in a modest bungalow with an atmosphere of misery, confusion and helplessness didn't make for a happy or healthy environment.

The one ray of sunshine being Agatha got her old job back working as a pharmacy assistant at St Thomas' Hospital in London. Best of all, it took her out of the house. Agatha couldn't wait to go to work, and Pimms grew weary being left alone with Margaret.

Months went by and Margaret grew weaker. Some things didn't change; letter writing between Agatha and Bea, and Agatha's passion for writing. She moved from short stories to mysteries. But were they any good and would they ever be published? Then it happened.

The chilling scream sent Agatha flying from her room. Pimms sat on Margaret's bed unable to speak. Agatha too couldn't speak. It's not every night your mother dies, and Pimms had now seen off two generations of mothers in the Vickery/Taylor family.

The doctor came, then the vicar and finally the undertaker.

'Do me a favour, Miss Agatha,' said Pimms when they had a moment alone. 'Outlive me if you please. I've discovered your mother and your grandmother dead in their bed. Well, no more, thank you. Feel free to swap roles. It's your turn to discover the dead.'

They looked at one another and, after a pause, they laughed—nothing loud or raucous, just a sprinkling of gallows' humour.

'Will you sell the house, Miss?' asked Pimms.

'Not tonight,' replied Agatha. She paused. 'And until I do, you will always have this place to call your home.'

Pimms turned teary. She had no family, home, investments or cash. The granddaughter owed her nothing.

Do they still have workhouses in London? Never mind; I'm safe and secure thanks to Agatha Crispie, the unknown divorcee.

'I suppose I'll have to call you, Madam now, Miss.'

Agatha thought about it. 'If you wish, Pimms, but don't you dare go and die on me until I say so.'

Genuine smiles appeared and a new chapter began in the lives of these two unusual women. Little did either know they would still be living in Teddington nearly two decades after the death of Agatha's mother.

Chapter 2

ARCHIBALD "ARCHIE" WALLOMAN WAS 62, widowed, wealthy and odd. He owned many shares in a Cornish mining company, and sat on the board as a senior partner. His father, Cuthbert Walloman, now deceased, was super rich and a bastard. He inherited money from *his* parents, married for aristocratic reasons, and sired "a few" children—but only one with his wife.

Mrs Cuthbert Walloman, the former Lavinia Trevallyn, enjoyed a sheltered and silver-spooned childhood being educated at home and a Swiss finishing school. Her marriage to Cuthbert could never be described as arranged. No, wait, it was exactly that. She and Cuthbert made a good pair both being self-absorbed, self-centred and self-opinionated. Their only child, Archibald, went off to boarding school not long after he could walk. The lad was a slow developer. He failed Oxbridge entrance exams, twice, and his mother refused to allow him to attend any other university. How could she explain to her circle of ladies who lunch in Belgravia, her son was studying at Salford or Sunderland?

So a place was found in the City for Archie and he surprised everyone by getting on. He married Penelope Squires, against his mother's express wishes, and a daughter was born named Elvira.

As Archie's business career blossomed, tragedy struck with his wife dying young from breast cancer. Elvira went to boarding and finishing school but spent a great deal of time with her widowed grandmother in her apartment in upmarket Belgravia. They became partners in snobbery and selfishness. Lavinia lived vicariously through her granddaughter, and Elvira starred as the spoilt brat.

The women became two peas in a pod and today, both lived on their father's country estate in Devonshire. As Elvira reached the debutant age, she and her grandmother spent forever plotting the course of marrying well. A royal husband was a runaway favourite with minor royals a satisfactory second choice. Leading aristocrats made up the fallback position.

Archie was kept well away from these manoeuvers, and all of his suggestions of golfing contacts and business associates were ignored. Whenever Archie recommended a chap he knew or worked with, the response was akin to a major tragedy.

'But he's in trade, father,' would be Elvira's immediate response.

'Stick to your business affairs, Archibald,' ordered his mother. 'Matters of marriage,'—note she didn't say "matters of the heart"— 'are well beyond your capabilities.' He got the message.

So having established who does what in the Walloman family seat, it should not be difficult to guess the response from Archie's mother and daughter when he announced he'd been thinking about getting married for a second time. Mind you, at the time, he had nobody in mind, but certainly the idea was alive and well.

In the Walloman country house, a fair way from the nearest village, and even a good stretch from the gatekeeper's cottage, a massive eruption took place. Lavinia and Elvira exploded.

'What!'

'How dare you!'

'Who is she?'

'You can't!'

'Over my dead body,' and much more was said, or rather shouted at Archie, and they were the kind and genuinely curious remarks.

This was a big mistake by the females because Archie had an ornery side and whenever his family ganged up on him, he would dig in his heels and fight back; pretty silly really because Lavinia and Elvira combined formed one powerful unit.

'Why?' yelled his daughter.

'If you stop yelling, I'll explain,' said her father.

'Who is she?' demanded his mother.

Archie explained. 'For years I've been embarrassed at work and golf club functions because I'm alone. All the other chaps have their wife in tow and I'm the sad-looking wallflower. People think there's something odd about me.'

'There *is* something odd about you,' snapped his loving mother although *loving* in this sentence is a misprint.

Archie explained his thinking. 'I need the flowers to be properly arranged, and dinner party planning to be expertly supervised. I need a companion who will support me and stand by my side. Neither of you can or will do those tasks so a wife is the perfect solution.'

'Have Mrs Beeton fill in,' ordered Lavinia.

'Don't be absurd, Mother. I refuse to be the senior partner of a major mining company who takes his cook and housekeeper to the Hunt Club Ball.'

'If you re-marry, Father, I'll disown you,' fired back Elvira.

'What's her status, her breeding?' demanded Lavinia.

Notice she had no interest in the name, age or qualities of this second wife-to-be. She wanted to know about her parents, have they any old world money—God we don't want any of that new money trash—and are they related to the King?

Archie slipped on his stubborn suit. Go Arch. 'I refuse to be browbeaten by anyone and most certainly not by my own family. If I do decide to re-marry, you will be advised at the appropriate time and in the appropriate manner.'

He made getting married sound like a motion to proceed at a board meeting.

His last speech took the wind out of the females' sails—for now. Archie walked from the room with nary an *Excuse me* or a *Goodbye*, and feeling pleased he had at least fired a warning shot across their bows.

Problem now, he thought, *is to find someone suitable, or rather anyone who is silly enough to marry me.*

Chapter 3

IT WAS 1919. The war to end all wars was over until the next war to end all wars began, and the two middle-aged women *always* met under the clock at London Waterloo. Everyone met there, and although a busy station, people found one another. Agatha arrived first—she liked being early—and felt a soft jab in her back. She turned to face her best friend, Beatrice Hopkiss. They'd been taking a holiday on the south coast every year for the last, oh, almost 20 years.

Each summer, Aggie and Bea booked the same B & B with Mrs Garston—ghastly Garston—in Bournemouth, and spent the days walking, talking and re-charging the batteries of their friendship.

Their embrace at Waterloo was strong and long. People rushed past. Workmen tackling yet another rebuild of the station hammered and whacked making all sorts of noise, and station announcements made the din a real smorgasbord of sound.

'We have twelve minutes before our train,' said Agatha. 'Do you fancy a cuppa before we go?'

'You know if I rush my tea I'll have to spend a penny on the train and you know how I hate the sight and sound of the sleepers whizzing past under my you know what.'

They laughed, picked up their own solitary suitcase and parasol and headed for the train. The locomotive had no lavatorial concerns, having already consumed its tea and bun in the form of water and coal, and full up it was too. The ladies chose third class. They couldn't afford first-class and second-class didn't exist. They found their seats.

Passengers in their compartment were of no consequence. Agatha and Bea would rabbit away non-stop and care not who heard their banter. As it happened, a stiff and starchy woman dressed entirely in black, who was a lot closer to the grave than the cradle, occupied one corner of the compartment. A stern young man with a bundle of papers sat beside her, and a middle-aged clergyman made up the party. The two female friends spoke to one another with their eyes.

'Fun lot they be,' whispered Bea and Agatha's eyebrows jiggled.

Their travel companions gave the women the once over and formed opinions, varying mind, on the two damsels.

Being in the cheap seats, their carriage was close to the locomotive and once the staff finished flag waving and whistle blowing, steam, smoke and grit sneaked into their compartment. Even with all unglazed windows and doors closed, you could still smell, even taste, the flavours of the engine. But smells aside, once underway, the ladies slipped into their serious gasbagging.

'So which of your wonderful sisters-in-law has stepped into the breach this time?' asked Agatha removing writing materials.

'Number Three,' replied Bea who referred to the wives of her three brothers by numbers.

'So only a modest all-in brawl required to get her to take the job,' smiled Agatha, and the other passengers' ears were pricked.

Bea whispered. 'Mother wanted my return date in writing.'

The women looked at one another. Agatha mouthed "No," in shock then shook her head in disbelief. Her mother had been "difficult" but Bea's was a shocker, a mixture of a sergeant-major and a dying swan.

As the women discussed the health of Bea's mother and Bea's life caring fulltime for her Ma, Agatha proved her skill at multi-tasking. She could converse with her friend and analyse the other passengers at the same time. Bea was used to this as Agatha opened a small notebook and scribbled ideas.

Elderly lady all in black either in permanent mourning or desperately trying to revive the Victorian era ... Young man with pages is either an author (like me) or a student revising his thesis ... Clergyman has been up to Lambeth Palace to see the Arch and is returning to his flock in the country.

All this note-taking was to help her create the characters who one day would populate her murder mysteries.

'So what news about the lovely gentleman?' asked Agatha. She referred to a bachelor who attended St Ethelbert's, the same church as Bea, and who seemed the only possible candidate for her hand. In a small village with few eligible males, and being chained to parental duties, everyone, including Bea herself, accepted that after twenty years of non-courtship, she was a shoo-in when it came to dying a spinster. No bridal dress required here, thank you.

Mind you, even if Mr Dinwiddie Whipple fancied Bea and decided to court her, being under petticoat government meant his expedition was over before it began. It was his mother's petticoat which ruled Dinwiddie and no woman was ever going to be good enough for her boy. He recently celebrated his 42nd birthday with Bea and Agatha not far behind. Celebrated is an incorrect choice of word because Mrs Whipple was not big on laughter, sucked lemons for a hobby, and of course regarded strong drink as evil.

The train chugged its way through the green and pleasant land heading south-west. The three passengers departed one at a time at Woking, Basingstoke and Southampton. With no additions, the friends were alone. Their regular letter-writing meant the latest news kept criss-crossing the country from Teddington to Tannington in Suffolk, but these trips, these holidays were the times to eyeball one another and dig to the bottom of subjects written about, to flesh out the subjects raised or only hinted at in correspondence. Now they could delve into the nitty-gritty of their lives.

Agatha spoke about her writing and her job working in a hospital dispensary in London but Bea knew all about those topics. The First World War had run its appalling course. Both women aged gracefully with Agatha living with her late mother's maid in Teddington, and Beatrice still caring for her mother in Suffolk.

Nothing thus far had been new or even remotely exciting until Agatha could stay her news no more. When she spoke it was a good thing they were alone because Bea's reaction would have startled the other passengers and surely frightened the horses.

'I've met a gentleman,' said Agatha and left it there. She knew there would be a top hat full of questions, more, but said nothing further giving her friend time to express her surprise, and then complain at not being told the earth-shattering news beforehand.

'You've what?' shouted Bea. 'We've been on this train for nearly two hours and only now you choose to tell me this monumental piece of news. How dare you Agatha Crispie!'

'I couldn't tell you before because there were passengers in our compartment.'

'So?'

'So? Look at yourself. I tell you my news and you've joined the circus complete with marching band. You would've terrified those passengers.'

Bea waved away Agatha's explanation. 'Stop making pathetic excuses, madam, and tell me everything.' Bea stared at Agatha with threatening eyes. 'And I mean *everything*.' She paused. 'Well come on, girl, what's his name? Is he wealthy? Where's he live? What's he do? And when will he ask you to marry him?'

Agatha felt warm inside thinking about her good news. She paused and then dropped an even bigger bombshell. 'He has already.'

Bea stalled then reacted physically, grabbed her friend's left hand and felt for an engagement ring finger beneath her glove. 'No ring. You little fibber. Is any of this true?'

'I'm to give him my answer when I return from our holiday.'

Bea changed in an instant. She cared deeply for her friend having seen first-hand how Agatha's first husband abandoned her. Bea was genuinely excited and happy, wary, but definitely pleased.

'Oh Aggie, this is wonderful news, wonderful.' She paused looking at her friend. 'Well, isn't it?'

Agatha took her time before she nodded. 'I hope so.'

She remembered her life nearly twenty years ago when she met Harry Crispie and fell madly in love. It was a case of her cup of happiness running over, certainly before the wedding, and for about a year thereafter. Then her life turned sour. She lost a baby and a husband. Agatha's heart was broken as the marriage she wanted ended and badly. Bea remembered everything. She helped Agatha change into her going-away outfit after the wedding reception and hugged her friend so hard. Alas Bea's wishes for Agatha's happiness were not enough.

Now, decades later, a second marriage proposal arrived out of the blue and naturally, Agatha became cautious. Bea didn't say it but she too worried lightning might strike the same place, person twice.

Alone in the compartment, Agatha gave Beatrice chapter and verse about the new romance in her life. Both women hoped love would be wonderful and long-lasting the second time around.

The train hammered along, Agatha described her new man, and Bea listened with great interest storing all sorts of questions.

'His name is Archie Walloman, Archibald actually, and he's older than me and lives in Devonshire in a large country house.'

'How much older?' asked Bea. She was ignored.

'He's a widower, well-off and part owns a mining company. This time, Bea, it's nothing like my relationship with Harry.'

Good thought Bea.

'We're not young or madly in love. This isn't the great romance. We're both looking for companionship as much as love. He goes to social and business functions and all the other gentlemen take their wife. Archie is all alone.'

'Poor thing,' said Bea in such a way Agatha didn't know if she meant it or was mocking her friend's new beau. Did Bea feel a tinge of jealousy at still being single, and sad at the prospect of spending less time with Agatha now her friend had a special man in her life?

'So what happened to Archie's first wife?' asked Bea.

'He's a widower.'

'You said that. But how did the first Mrs Walloman die?' She whispered. 'Come on, you're the mystery writer. Was she poisoned? Did hubby do her in?'

Agatha gave a wee smile. She was glad her news was "out". She needed to share it with Bea but wanted to do so in person, and only when Agatha was sure it was going to happen.

'The marriage would certainly suit me, Bea. I gain companionship, hopefully love, and the freedom to write. I'll live in a big house with servants, and a wealthy husband means I can forget housework and bills, and concentrate on my dream of becoming a writer.'

Sounds great; what's the catch? thought Bea. 'How did you meet?'

Agatha smiled, thinking about Archie and how their relationship began. 'He comes up to London on business about once a month. He came to the hospital to visit a sick colleague and was lost. I was walking back to the pharmacy and he asked for directions.'

'And that was it? Love at first sight in the corridors of St Thomas' Hospital?' She mimicked the man she hadn't met. 'Excuse me, madam—did he call you Miss?—can you direct me to hospital Reception please, oh, and by the way, will you marry me?'

Agatha laughed. 'Not exactly; after work I was walking to the station in the rain. Archie came out of a shop and we both had umbrellas and collided. He apologized, we recognized one another. Across the road was a coffee shop, and he invited me to tea.' Agatha smiled. 'We had a lovely time getting to know one another.'

Bea sounded hurt. 'Don't tell me he proposed over a Devonshire tea?'

'Don't be silly. He asked for my phone number which proved tricky.'

'Oh?'

'I was out when he rang and Pimms answered.'

'Is that old biddy still alive?'

'I'd told her nothing about Archie and she carried on talking about me in the third person.'

'The what?'

Agatha imitated Pimms who sometimes would use her toffy voice. 'I regret Madam is not at home, sir. May one take a message?'

Agatha laughed remembering Archie thought he'd rung a stately home and not a bungalow in Teddington. Bea forced a smile still feeling miffed this major piece of news had only just been revealed.

'Why didn't you tell me all this before?' she whined.

'Oh Bea, you of all people must surely understand. I couldn't believe any man would show an interest in me after all these years.

We're middle-aged my dear, and for me it's worse, I'm a divorcee. I had to be sure it was going to happen before I broadcast anything.'

Bea nodded. Agatha spoke the truth. 'Have you met his family?'

'Not yet. And that's one thing I'm a little worried about.'

'Oh dear, that sounds ominous.'

'I have the feeling they're not happy Archie plans to re-marry.'

'Who are *they*?'

'His mother's a widow and his daughter a spinster, and they both live with Archie in the family home in the country.'

'Well no wonder they don't want to meet you.' Agatha looked surprised. 'You're the enemy. You'll dethrone the matriarch and pinch the daughter's inheritance.'

Agatha objected. 'Oh Bea, don't be awful. Besides, it can't be true. Yes, Archie has money but I'm an independent woman.'

'Who plans living in a country house with a maid called Pimms.'

They both smiled coming down from the emotional high of Agatha's news.

'And love,' said Bea; 'where does love sit in this relationship?'

'I told you, at my age one can't be fussy when it comes to accepting a marriage proposal. It's the truth, my girl; we're both in the beggars-can't-be-choosers camp. It's cruel but it's true.'

Bea nodded. She agreed then turned to other questions. 'We can come back to love but tell me about his proposal. Was it romantic?'

Agatha hesitated and Bea worried. She saw up close and personal the pain her friend suffered when husband number one treated her appallingly. Neither woman wanted a repeat performance.

'If you mean a candlelit dinner, roses and the moon above then no, it wasn't romantic.' If Agatha was honest, it was more like a business merger between two lonely adults. 'Let's just say he behaved impeccably and promised me a comfortable life wanting for nothing.'

The sting went out of their conversation. Agatha's news was a conversation stopper and while both thought of the future, it was easy for both to think back and wonder if marriage number 2 would have a happy ending.

This latest holiday was different. They enjoyed one another's company, of course they did, but a cloud hung over the week. Jokes were fewer and less punchy. Giggling slipped down the popularity ladder. Even complaints about Mrs Garston, the landlady and her cooking, were few and far between.

The next afternoon, the women sat on the beachfront and Bea pulled the trigger.

'So are you going to accept Archie's proposal?'

'Yes,' said Agatha without feeling or emotion.

'I hope you're going to invite your best friend to the wedding.'

Agatha frowned and snapped. 'Don't be silly, Bea. If you're not there, there'll *be* no wedding.'

Bea squeezed her friend's arm and decided to ask more questions.

'So what will you do with your cottage?'

'Archie says I should sell it. He knows a few first-rate estate agents and thinks I should put the money into government bonds.'

'Don't,' said Bea. Agatha looked shocked. 'Keep it as an investment and as a bolt hole in time of need.'

They looked at one another. Bea didn't have to refer to Harry Crispie and his fling with his Portsmouth floozy. Agatha knew.

'Look Bea, I know you mean well but I'm not some flibbertigibbet. I've been married. I know what's involved. My parents are dead and I'm on my own. I want to make a go of this writing business and I don't want to finish up an old maid living alone in an empty cottage.'

'Like me you mean?'

That hurt. Agatha would rather die than upset her friend. But it sounded bad. Now they were arguing. In the past it would be about where they'd go for tea or how much they'd spend on hats. Not now.

'That's not fair, Bea. You shouldn't twist my words. If you told me you were engaged to be married, my first and only wish would be happiness for you and your future husband.'

Bea felt a tad ashamed. She didn't need to apologise. Her face spoke volumes and the way she squeezed her friend's hand reinforced her true feelings.

They sat and watched the waves before Bea changed the topic of conversation. She didn't want to dissuade her friend from this

24

marriage but rather, make sure Agatha had thought about all the possible problems. To be forewarned is to be forearmed.

'You know your new stepdaughter is going to resent you.'

'How can you say that? Elvira and I might become best friends.'

Bea felt pain. *She* was Agatha's best friend and spoke from the heart. 'My darling girl,' she said. 'You are about 20 years younger than your new husband. Chances are he will die before you, even well before you.' Agatha felt her heart beat faster. 'Archie's daughter will think her father's money will be coming to her.'

'As it should do and will.'

'But have you and Archie discussed your wills?'

Agatha fell silent. She expected her friend to celebrate her news, to be happy, and ask how she might help with the wedding, moving house, even in choosing the honeymoon venue. Instead she raised embarrassing topics which had nothing to do with her. Agatha took a deep breath and, despite being annoyed with Bea and her questions, deep inside, she knew her friend meant well and spoke the truth.

'Bea,' she said, 'I've thought long and hard about all that could happen, and I've made what I hope is the right decision. Now can we please talk about something else?'

Bea stood and offered her arm. 'Then good for you. Now come on, it's down to the pier and back before Mrs Garston's dreaded stew.'

They set off both knowing the other's thoughts. Bea still wanted to help if she could, and tried to make her next question a simple, matter-of-fact query. 'What's going to happen with your maid?'

'She'll be coming with me. I told Archie she's been with the family forever and he agreed.'

'He agreed?'

'Well he grunted and I assumed that meant he approved.'

'How will she fit in with Archie's family?'

'Oh you know, Pimms; she puts up with and fits in with everyone.'

They headed home with Bea more worried than ever about her friend's forthcoming nuptials. *Yes, but will they put up with her?*

Chapter 4

AGATHA MET STEPDAUGHTER, Elvira and mother-in-law, Lavinia at their home a week before the wedding. It was the beginning of August with sunshine aplenty. Had the atmosphere in the elegant sitting room been any more chilly, frost would have formed on the *inside* of the spacious windows. Archie brought up innocuous topics of conversation to cover the resentment his family directed as much at him as his future bride.

Agatha had doubts. She could hardly miss the thinly-disguised hostility towards the future Mrs Walloman. It gave her a sleepless night. She spent it in the guest wing of the Walloman country house, a manor house in all but name. She wondered if Archie might come a-calling when the house had gone a-bed. Nothing. Of an eager would-be groom came there none. Was he religious, incapable, nervous or not interested?

In the morning, Archie took her for a walk in the grounds assuring her Elvira and Lavinia would come round once she and Archie were wed. Archie's selling skills were poor. He excelled in business but less so when dealing with women. In fact he failed intimacy. Was she about to marry her father?

Agatha adored the magnificent house, her new home, and the glorious grounds. A man tending the garden raised his cap as Archie and Agatha passed by. 'Mornin' Sir, Ma'am,' he said. Archie nodded.

'We have only one gardener,' said Archie. 'Any more and they slacken off.'

'But it's such a large garden. Can he manage on his own?'

Archie ignored her question. He ignored any difficult question.

'You'll be in charge of the flowers, Agatha. You decide which ones go in which rooms. You can have your maid, Timms pick them but arranging will be your domain.'

Her mind raced. *Do I really know this man?* She ran through the pros and cons. *Am I setting myself up to fail?*

She wanted companionship and the freedom to write. If Archie wanted her, that was enough. Why should two disgruntled relatives bully and prevent her doing what she wanted to do? She wasn't in love or, at her age, blinded by someone wealthy, or even by anyone wanting her as their wife. Her thinking was clear.

You only live once, girl. Get out there and make life happen.

She wasn't expecting any other marriage proposals, and wondered what her parents would think of their only daughter, the bookworm and possible poet and novelist becoming the Lady of the Manor.

As far as nuptials go, this wasn't the wedding of the year. Agatha didn't have a family, and Archie's daughter and mother stayed home. Archie phoned the night before. 'Mother is not up to travelling and Elvira fell from her horse when out riding. Bruising only but we can't be too careful with possible broken bones and concussion,' said Archie. Agatha didn't believe in omens but if she did, having her new husband's family avoid the wedding raised a red flag—more like two.

The ceremony took place in the Marylebone Registry Office in London and they were couple number five on the day. It was about as small a wedding party as one could find.

Archie's best man was one of his business associates, a chap he played golf with once nearly five years ago. Archie had described Carruthers to Agatha as his best pal and long-time golfing partner. This "best pal" was the fourth chap Archie had asked, the first three having said "No" without hesitation or excuse. The groom's failed social skills applied to both sexes.

Agatha didn't need to ask anyone to be her Maid of Honour. Miss Beatrice Hopkiss was a given. The week before the wedding, Bea came to stay in Teddington. Pimms found herself in the way as she assumed the Maid of Honour tasks were mundane and should therefore be performed by her.

'Pimms,' said Agatha, 'I'm ever so grateful for everything you've done and want to do but this time I want you to take a break.'

'A break, Madam? Whatever can you mean?'

'A holiday, Pimms; I want you to go on holiday.'

Pimms' face registered nothing. She genuinely wasn't sure what Madam was speaking about. 'I don't think I've ever been on one of those, Madam, at least not that I can remember.'

Agatha explained, leaving Pimms more hurt than happy. 'But it's your wedding next week, Madam. How can I help if I'm not here?'

'You don't need to be here, Pimms.' This brought more confusion for Pimms. 'Look, my first wedding was small and this is smaller. Bea helped me prepare before and wants to and can do so again.'

Pimms looked stunned. 'But I'll have nothing to do, Madam.' She had little to do anyway.

'Indeed you will. Listen, I remember you talking about growing up in Yorkshire, and how you've never been back there since Queen Victoria became Empress of India.'

'Did I say that?'

'I have a gift for you, Pimms. It's a first-class return ticket from London to Yorkshire with a week's accommodation in the Swan Hydro, a spa in Harrowgate. You can visit places where you grew up.'

Pimms now understood and a smile crept over her face. 'Oh, how wonderful, Madam; thank you, thank you so very much.'

'Everything is booked in my name, Miss Agatha Taylor. I could have booked in your name but I'm embarrassed to admit I don't know your other name.'

'I have only one, Madam; Pimms, as in Smike of Dotheboys Hall.'

Agatha and Bea were impressed and an envelope was handed to the maid. 'Now I want you to pack a bag, Pimms and when you come home, you can pack again for your new life in Devonshire in your huge new quarters. You're to be the maid to the Lady of the Manor.'

Still in shock, Pimms spoke. 'Oh, Madam, I hardly know which way to turn.'

'At the front gate you turn to the left, take the train from Teddington to Waterloo, the 68 bus to Kings Cross, and from there the train to Yorkshire.'

Speechless but excited, Pimms left, leaving the Bride and Maid of Honour to discuss important matters. Bea began.

'Father asked if you wanted him to give you away again,' said Bea.

Agatha reacted. 'Alas I think the registry office has a table and chairs with nary a pew or pipe organ in sight. But please thank him.'

'With his rheumatism, you might have been walking him.'

Agatha went to her bureau and took out a package. She opened it and removed its contents. 'I've bought a negligee,' she said.

'A what?' asked Bea, genuinely ignorant of such an item.

Agatha held it against her body. 'It's this thin, silk dressing gown. You wear it over your nightie.'

'But how on Earth does it keep you warm at night?'

'I think it's more a fashion for passion garment. It's supposed to encourage your husband to keep *you* warm.'

'Oh,' said Bea. 'Well it's no good asking me about that sort of thing. I still have my virginal Victorian nightgowns.'

Still Agatha persisted. 'Do you think, at my age, it'll make me look a bit desperate? Am I Agatha, the mutton dressed as lamb bride?'

'I told you, Aggie, until Dinwiddie Whipple sweeps me off my feet, I'll continue to know a bit about sheep, chutney and the Book of Common Prayer but absolutely nothing about sex.'

They looked at one another then laughed, then laughed a lot.

'So how is dear old Dinwiddie these days?' asked Agatha.

'Gormless. Actually his ma is poorly and if she dies I'll move.'

'Move? You? Whatever for?'

'Without his tyrannical mother, Dinwiddie would be free to go courting. Now can you imagine being seduced by Mr Whipple? It'd be the blind leading the blind. He'd need a book with illustrations, a miner's lamp and a magnifying glass.'

Their laughter resumed with much more power. They ribbed one another about men, seduction and poor old Dinwiddie. Their joking faded and Bea steered towards safer ground.

'So you've settled on Scotland for your honeymoon,' said Bea. 'I think it's nice this time of year.'

'It is but I think Archie's getting cold feet.'

Bea blanched. 'What! Not about the wedding?'

'No, about Scotland. One of his companies is facing a takeover bid and he doesn't want to be hundreds of miles away if he's needed.'

Bea was in a quandary. She had a few concerns about her dear friend's decision to marry this man, and this latest news about scrapping the honeymoon only added to her pessimism. She wanted to say what she felt but hated the thought of hurting Agatha.

She thought. Maybe I'm wrong. Maybe this marriage is right for both of them. What should I do? Nothing, because what do I know?

'A penny for them,' said Agatha looking at her friend. Bea lied.

'Oh, I was trying to guess Pimms' other name, and who would have known she was a fan of Dickens?'

Agatha nodded and grimaced. 'I'll never be a Dickens,' she said. 'But I would love to write murder mysteries, stories to engage readers with whodunit endings people can never or hardly ever guess.'

'So what's stopping you?'

'Oh, being stuck in a small bungalow with an elderly maid who wants to care for me like she did for my grandmother when my grandmother lived in a rambling old mansion and everyone in that type of house in that era had a butler, maid, cook and a footman.'

Bea looked at her friend. 'So that's why you're keen on the marriage to the wealthy mining magnate. You want a big house with a place for Pimms, servants and a space for your writing to flourish.'

Agatha nodded. 'You're pretty close to the truth, Miss Beatrice Hopkiss. And do you think that's such a bad thing?'

Bea paused. 'No, not at all, and above all I want you to be happy.'

Agatha folded her new negligee and placed it back in its box. 'You always were the perceptive type, Bea. But now I need my beauty sleep, girlie. Believe it or not, I'm getting married in the morning.'

For Agatha's second wedding, London turned on a typical summer's day—non-stop rain. Middlesex v Essex at Lords was abandoned without a ball being bowled. Agatha and Bea took an age to dress, fix their hair and apply their make-up. When ready, they put on raincoats and boots with their shoes safe and dry in a bag. Agatha's small packed suitcase for the honeymoon, including her new negligee, waited expectantly beside the front door. When they opened that door, the rain increased as if daring them to venture forth.

'Hang the expense,' said Agatha. 'We'll go by cab.'

And they did; two women, two umbrellas and one small suitcase.

'I'll do the carrying,' said Bea taking Agatha's case.

Dodging the drops and worrying about their shoes and stockings, the ladies entered the registry office. Archie stood there looking distressed. The groom was nervous. Not a good start.

'Hello Archie,' said Agatha. 'This is my best friend, Bea.'

He tried to smile and nod but failed. Surely he would give his bride-to-be a kiss and compliment the ladies on their outfits. He did neither and his opening remark was unusual.

'Have you seen Carruthers?' Archie spoke of his best pal and long-time golfing partner, the one he barely knew. 'Damn fellow's late.'

Female hearts fluttered not from excitement but fear. Archie's family chose not to attend and now his best man had done a bunk. The portents of a long and happy marriage pushed Agatha to worry.

An official approached. 'Could I have the name please?'

'Walloman,' snapped Archie with a face like thunder. 'And I can't find the best man.'

'Not to worry, sir,' said the official, calm and experienced. 'We have a witness for such an emergency. Today it's Mr Whipple.'

The women looked at one another in horror. It can't be. Dinwiddie had never been more than 10 miles from Tannington. His only suit was a handmade hand-me-down. To have him in the wedding party would be the ultimate insult.

Relief rained down when Mr Gordon Whipple of Maida Vale was introduced minutes before the ceremony. He was only a few years older than Archie but looked 103.

He knew his lines and signed his name with a flourish. Archie did kiss Agatha when the official declared them to be man and wife, and gave Gordon a small tip after which the bride and groom and Matron of Honour hightailed it out into the rain.

So it was a wedding breakfast for three. Lunch at the Savoy would be nice or at the Ritz. After all, it's not every day you get married even with a stand-in best man, and being the second time round for both bride and groom. But we're dealing with Archibald Walloman here and so the groom bundled the women into The Queens Arms where they did a nice bangers and mash with a pint and a G & T for the ladies, at 5/6d a head. Big spender was Archie.

Agatha's first wedding featured a drunken best man and her second a missing best man. Life couldn't get worse—or could it?

'Now Agatha, my dear,' said Archie, 'I'm afraid the takeover bid is getting serious and I need to get home as soon as possible. We can have our honeymoon once matters settle down.' He looked at his watch. 'So if we hurry, we can catch the 2.21.'

'But Archie, I only have my small suitcase. Everything else is back at Teddington.'

'Don't worry, my dear. I'm sure your friend Beau here can send whatever it is you need.'

Beau, in real life, Bea, needed no more convincing her friend had made a ghastly mistake in marrying this man but kept her own counsel for the sake of her friend, the blushing, or was she now the rushing bride? After all, the die was cast and the horse had bolted.

Agatha was wondering what she might wear on her wedding night. Her paisley woollen dressing gown was hanging behind the door in her bedroom in Teddington. It looked like the negligee might make an appearance after all. *Was that Archie's plan all along?*

So Beau, a.k.a. Bea, hugged her friend and shook hands with the groom. The newlyweds scampered off to Paddington with Beatrice waving and wondering when her friend's clothes and maid would eventually, if ever, make it to the West Country. Bea had the short trip to Teddington before her return to Suffolk and to the dopey Dinwiddie the next day.

Has any bride ever had such a beginning to her marriage?

Chapter 5

ARCHIE ESCORTED AGATHA from the train at Torquay. She felt foolish being dressed to the nines for her wedding and carrying a bouquet while Archie carried her case. *Everyone is looking at me.*

He led her to a horse and carriage standing outside the station. A man stood beside the vehicle and, as the couple approached, he opened a door. Agatha thought she'd seen him before. She had. It was the gardener at Ashpaddock, the man who doffed his cap when Archie took Agatha for a tour of the grounds.

The man doffed his cap again. 'Good day to you Sir, Ma'am,' he said as Archie helped or rather shepherded Agatha into the carriage.

'Quick as you can, Weeding,' ordered Archie, and the bridal couple headed home. Rather than point out important and interesting places to his new bride as they travelled, Archie read a business report firmly indicating his priorities in life; business first and wife, further down the list. In Archie's case, she was much further down the list.

'They're coming Grandmother,' called Elvira who had been on patrol all afternoon.

'Is she in the carriage?' called Lavinia reclining in her favourite chair. Of all the furniture in her home in Belgravia, she brought only two armchairs and woe betide anyone who sat in either.

'I think so.'

'What do you mean, think so?'

'It looks like she's wearing a Tam o'Shanter.'

Lavinia was genuinely shocked. 'Oh my God, she's Scottish and was married wearing a Tam o'Shanter! Heaven help us.'

'It might be a turban. And I can't see the maid. Maybe she's not coming after all.'

'Good. Now listen carefully, Elvira. We must stand together against this woman. Your father has made a ghastly mistake and this new wife must be kept in her place. Do you understand?'

'Oh I understand, Grandmother.' Elvira stared through the window then recoiled in shock. 'She has only one suitcase.'

'One suitcase and a funny hat? What is she, a gypsy?'

'Here they come.' Elvira hurried to her spot on the expensive French settee. Both women preened waiting for the door to the large sitting room to open. Their preening hurt.

'Take Mrs Wallowan's suitcase to her bedroom,' said Archie to the housekeeper, Mrs Beeton.

'*Her* bedroom,' whispered an enraged Elvira.

'*I'm* Mrs Wallowman,' fumed Lavinia as both women faced front when the door opened.

'Ah, there you are,' said Archie leading Agatha into the room. 'Now you'll be pleased to know Agatha and I were wed in a lovely service in London. There were chairs, Mother, so you would have been able to attend and sit after all.'

Lavinia put on her fake sadness face. 'Oh how disappointing. I was so looking forward to being there.' Her lie was intended to lay down a marker, to set the standard—begin as you mean to go on.

Elvira joined the charade. 'Me too of course, Father and Stepmother, but having to care for Grandmother is so important.'

Agatha overlooked the sarcasm and played a straight bat. This fooled her new relatives, at least for now. Was she being honest or mimicking them?

'How are your bruises?' asked Agatha of her stepdaughter.

'Pardon?' replied Elvira as Archie winced.

'Your father said you took a tumble when out riding.'

'Oh *those* bruises. I'd show them to you only they're in a delicate spot.' The resultant silence had teeth.

'Well, Agatha,' said Archie wanting to separate the three women in his life before the second world war began not far from Torquay; why don't you unpack and dress for dinner?'

'Dress for dinner?' said Agatha in shock.

'Oh we always dress for dinner,' said Lavinia staring at her new daughter-in-law, the one she hated.

'Always,' said Elvira with feeling.

'But we had to cancel the honeymoon,' said Agatha.

'Postpone,' corrected Archie.

'And most of my clothes are back in Teddington,' added Agatha.

'Teddington,' said Lavinia in such a way her mouth needed a good dose of soap and water.

'Why don't you dine in your new bedroom,' suggested Elvira. 'We would understand.'

'Nonsense,' said Archie actually standing up for his bride. There's a first time for everything. 'Tonight we'll dress as we are.' His family wanted to scream as Archie opened the door and Agatha took the hint and left.

With the door closed, both women hissed their objections.

'That is the thin edge of the wedge, Archibald,' spat his mother.

'Standards, Father, we must maintain standards,' added his daughter. 'And where's her maid?'

'And why would a woman from Teddington have a maid?' asked his mother.

Archie clapped his hands once. The women fell silent as their rage smoldered. 'Enough! Agatha is now my wife and you will treat her with the courtesy she deserves. Whether you like it or not, she is now the lady of the house. You don't have to love her.'

'Love her?' whined Lavinia. 'It's impossible to even like her.'

'How can you say that?' demanded Archie. 'Give her a chance.'

'Why should we love her? *You* don't,' fired back Elvira.

Her father paused but treated Elvira's remark with contempt. He continued. 'Or even like her but you will respect her position.' He paused. 'Do I make myself clear?'

Silence.

'Good, then I shall see you both, wearing those clothes, when next the gong sounds for dinner.' He left and their eyes narrowed, and their rage bubbled on a low heat.

The dining room was large with a table to match, meaning the four diners were miles apart. Intimate conversation with the new and despised stepmother was unlikely to happen anyway. So whatever words were spoken had to be *forte* plus. It's rude to shout.

'Agatha and I will take our honeymoon as soon as this takeover bid is defeated. We're thinking of going to Scotland,' said the patriarch.

'I've heard New Zealand is rather lovely at this time of year,' suggested Elvira, 'especially the South Island.'

'New Zealand is lovely at *any* time of the year,' added Lavinia.

Archie ignored the suggestions. 'Now, Agatha's maid will be joining us next month and ...'

'Next week,' corrected Agatha. 'I should have told you, Archie. Due to the missing luggage, I've asked her to bring my goods on Monday.'

Archie acquiesced. 'She'll be a big help for Mrs Beeton. Simms will be Agatha's maid but I will allow her to help you, Elvira and of course, you too Mother.'

'Does she have suitable references?' asked Lavinia.

'Over sixty years' service in my family,' replied Agatha.

'Of course it's not the years of service but the class of the referee,' said Lavinia looking straight at her new daughter-in-law.

Archie tried to prevent the outbreak of open warfare, working hard to place nondescript topics on the conversation agenda. 'Agatha is keen on her hobby of reading and I have suggested she spends time in the library.'

'I use the library every day,' said Lavinia.

'So do I,' added Elvira.

'Well it's a large room and I'm sure there is space for everyone,' announced the patriarch. Had he ever been an umpire before?

Agatha decided to join the discussion. 'It's not only my interest in reading, Archie. I'm especially keen on writing and have a dream of one day becoming a published author.'

The other women coughed, even groaned, and the subsequent silence oozed disbelief, silent laughter and mockery. Lavinia and Elvira lined up to have a pop at belittling the new member of the family—not a blood relation, of course.

Lavinia objected. 'I go to the library for peace and quiet. Any form of noise such as scratchy writing and loud turning of pages will ruin my relaxation time.'

'I agree,' said Elvira. 'And what is the point of writing something which is never published?'

'Or likely to *be* published,' added Lavinia.

Archie's plan for peace was failing—badly and quickly. 'I'm sure Agatha can write softly. Isn't that so, Agatha?'

The new wife was in no doubt. Archie's mother and daughter were out to make her life a misery. But no way was she going to roll over, and so fired back at her now clearly defined enemies.

'I can indeed. But before I write, I need to conduct research; I need to plot my novels and then plan my next sentence. For that I need the typical silence of a library; no talking, coughing or rustling of dresses.' Well said, Aggie.

Oh dear. The situation seemed to be heading towards pistols at dawn with the team of grandmother and granddaughter spoiling for a fight. But it was good to see Agatha not allowing the bullies to do their worst and escape a counter-attack. Archie struggled to keep his temper.

'I suggest we try and be civil about this,' he said. 'Agatha will use the library to read and write, and Mother and Elvira will use the library to sew and relax and meditate or whatever it is you do.' He looked at all three. If looks could kill! 'And that is my final word.'

Agatha now saw her marriage as a war of attrition.

Chapter 6

PIMMS ARRIVED BY TRAIN with her small case containing all her worldly belongings, plus Agatha's large trunk. Weeding the gardener cum driver strained his back lifting then tying the trunk to the back of the carriage. Archie came out when they arrived at Ashpaddock and gave limited help and only as far as the verandah. 'Agatha, I suggest you open your trunk, and have Bimms carry your clothes upstairs.'

'I hope I packed everything, Madam,' said Pimms.

'I'm sure you did, Pimms. And how was Yorkshire?'

The maid slipped back into the accent of her youth. 'Oh aye, lass, you were reight, it were champion.'

Lavinia and Elvira peered through the sitting room windows hiding behind the velvet curtains.

'Are they certain the maid is actually alive?' asked Lavinia.

'I wish I could see inside her trunk,' said Elvira.

'Why? What interest could you possibly have in cheap and tatty, unfashionable clothes and trinkets?'

Mrs Beeton gave Agatha and Pimms a hand, and between the three women, Agatha's bits and bobs were settled in her room.

Agatha took Pimms to show her the room set aside for the maid. It was much bigger than her shoebox in Teddington.

'I felt sad leaving your bungalow, Madam. Can you not rent it?'

'I can, Pimms, but first I want to see how life pans out in my role as Mrs Walloman.'

Pimms reacted quickly and with unexpected anger. 'He's not been cruel to you, Madam?'

'No, Pimms. But his mother and daughter are yet to show me the slightest kindness. To them I am the unwanted interloper.'

'I don't know what that means, Madam, but if any of them tries it on, you tell me and I'll give any or all of them a taster.'

'Actually I think I've married my father, Pimms.'

'Oh?'

'Mr Walloman is incapable of affection and afraid of intimacy.'

Pimms pondered. 'I think that might be a little bit of too much information, Madam. I'll choose a "no comment" if you don't mind.'

Agatha laughed. 'Now, here's a word to the wise, Pimms. Mr Walloman's bark is much worse than his bite. However, his mother and daughter hated and opposed me before I arrived and, since I arrived, they've upped the ante.'

'You've lost me there again, Madam.'

'They want me out and, by extension, you as well.'

'Right, well as I said, let 'em try, Madam; just let 'em try.'

'So I hope I can rely on you, Pimms, to be quiet and polite and the meekest of humble domestic servants.'

Pimms pondered. 'I fear you're going to be disappointed, Madam.'

Agatha wasn't disappointed at all. She knew Pimms' reputation ever since, as a child, Agatha went to visit her grandmother. Pimms and Agatha's grandmother used to send sparks flying. The maid didn't know how to take a backward step. Let battle commence.

In the library, the War of the Posers was on for young and old. Agatha liked writing there. She had easy access to books—Archie's grandmother had been a literary lady and built a wonderful book collection. She would have been delighted to see her library, for the first time in ages, being used as it was intended to be used.

Agatha would research her latest mystery and then tackle the task of creating a masterpiece—well, something half decent.

At first, Pimms played the snobbish women at their own game. Lavinia and Elvira would ring a small bell and summon Pimms asking her for a drink, or to have a curtain closed an inch, or to check with Mrs Beeton as to the day's luncheon menu. They spoke with exaggerated accents pretending to be upper upper-class persons.

After a while, Pimms began to impersonate them. The bell would tinkle, Pimms would appear and address the matriarch.

'You rang, Madam?' drawled Pimms in a flat monotone.

'The sun is too bright. Close that curtain three and a half inches,' sneered Lavinia.

'Certainly, Madam,' said Pimms moving in her affected way. Whenever she walked in front of Lavinia and Elvira, and thus could be seen by the two women, Pimms would add a small limp to her gait. It used to disgust Lavinia and Elvira but amuse Agatha no end who could watch everything from her desk in the corner of the library.

To annoy the snobs, Pimms would switch the limp from one leg to the other. Lavinia and Elvira were sure she was limping on her left leg yesterday but today it was her right. Agatha was close to tears watching her maid mock the people who mocked her.

But all this did nothing to help have Agatha's writing accepted. She read published mystery writers to try and capture their tricks of plotting, creating interesting characters, writing clever and appropriate dialogue and best of all, fooling or teasing the reader as to whodunit.

The major problem being that without being published, there were no readers to appreciate her tales.

The promised honeymoon never eventuated—no surprise there—and Pimms continued being treated with contempt, which meant Agatha's writing career stalled. Literary agents and publishers rejected her offerings. She made a decision. She would work harder and longer. This meant rising earlier than Lavinia and Elvira, and working alone and uninterrupted in the library.

With the rest of the house still abed, Agatha would settle in the library and write. The early bird gets the germ of their novel and makes progress. The days then weeks went by and Agatha finally saw some results. Her mysteries multiplied. She kept her writing silent, and Pimms kept her response times acceptable.

But the present routine couldn't last. Lavinia and Elvira pushed Pimms to bursting point. Something or someone was bound to crack.

One morning, Agatha again rose early and began revising her latest mystery. Being alone in the library, she was able to speak aloud and often did as she wrote.

'Oh no, Inspector, I'm ... sure ... it ... was ... weed killer.' She stopped writing and crossed out the words weed killer. 'No, it's far too obvious.' She left her desk, headed for the bookshelves, and located the book on poisons. There were so many books on so many subjects. *Was Archie's grandmother a writer of mysteries?*

Turning to the index, she found the chapter listing a variety of poisons. 'It must be exotic.' She read the list. 'Now with my experience working in a pharmacy, I should know which is perfect for my murder.' She read aloud. 'Arsenic, cyanide, warfarin ...'

Her research was interrupted by a person in the corridor.

'Agatha!' rumbled Lavinia.

This was the routine most mornings with Lavinia attention seeking, making demands for service and generally being a right royal pain in the backside. As per usual, Agatha ignored her mother-in-law, and kept reading aloud. '... ricin, strychnine, hemlock.'

The octogenarian toddler, now petulant child, became violent and struck the door with her walking-stick. 'Agatha!' she snarled.

The writer took a deep breath and called, placing an emphasis on every word. 'The ... door ... is ... open.'

Lavinia pretended not to hear. 'Unlock this door immediately.' Agatha did nothing so the wilful toddler spat the dummy and whacked the door repeatedly with her stick; bang, bang, bang.

Shaking her head, Agatha replaced the book, walked sensibly to the now bruised but unlocked door and opened it with ease. She stood back leaving the infuriated widow framed in the doorway. Agatha made a sweeping gesture inviting Lavinia to enter.

'Abracadabra,' said Agatha and waited for the Grande dame to move. Using her stick for support, unnecessarily so, Lavinia affected a much offended walk and "strode" across the library towards her chair. Should anyone even think of sitting in Lavinia's chair, transportation to the Colonies was the least one could expect.

Agatha closed the door and returned to her desk to work on the exotic poison. She had her back to Lavinia who stopped a foot from her chair and spoke to no-one. It was a simple statement of fact.

'My chair has been moved.'

Steam seeped from her ears. Agatha ignored the prima donna who, enraged, thumped her stick, hissing. 'My chair has been moved.'

Agatha could take no more. 'I heard you the first time, Mrs Walloman. Now if you don't mind, I'm trying to work.'

Lavinia spoke softly but loud enough for Agatha to hear. 'Ha. A woman who works is a domestic.'

Now the volume became lively.

'And I'll thank you to not strike the furniture,' fired back Agatha.

'I'll strike whatever I like. This is my son's house.'

'And I am your son's wife, the lady of the house.'

The volume dropped as the contempt kicked in.

'Divorcee!' growled Lavinia who lowered herself into the chair which in fact *had* been moved. It was a prank played by Pimms who wanted to annoy the matriarch as much as possible. Every two or three days, the wicked maid would sneak into the library at night and rearrange Madame's chair a little solely to annoy the hell out of her.

'Witch!' mumbled Agatha sotto voce.

Now Lavinia turned to face her foe. '*I* am the senior Mrs Walloman and my status entitles me to respect; a quality I find singularly lacking in this house.'

Agatha gave as good as she got, her volume on a slow crescendo. 'Oh there's plenty of respect, Mother-in-law. Respect for furniture, silence, privacy and the *right to work*.'

Lavinia fumed and seethed. 'Women do not work!'

Agatha lost the anger in her arguing and switched to sarcasm. 'Oh dear, haven't you heard, Mother-in-law? Queen Victoria's dead. A wife is no longer a husband's possession or a part of his property!'

Lavinia hated her daughter-in-law for several reasons, not least being that Agatha was right. Giving up this latest fight, she reached for the small bell on the table beside her chair. The bell rang— impatiently. Lavinia had the ability to transmit emotion through inanimate objects. She received no response which annoyed the matriarch who was used to obtaining immediate service whenever she demanded same. Annoyed—still—she rang again.

Agatha wanted to dong the woman. 'There is no need to keep ringing; Pimms has excellent hearing.' And, as if on cue, the door opened and Pimms arrived. She strolled towards Lavinia.

When it came to clothing, Pimms was a traditionalist, wearing the same black dress, white apron and white headpiece she wore when attending to Agatha's grandmother and mother. Strangely, Lavinia approved although would never admit the fact.

Pimms sniffed. 'You rang, m'Lady?'

Lavinia regarded looking at the servants as both a mortal sin and an appalling social faux pas. 'Tea,' she said.

Pimms was sick of the routine of being summoned and continually asked the same thing. She decided to mix the conversation up a bit.

'Tea? Are you sure, Madam? What's wrong with a sherry?'

Lavinia looked like she'd been slapped. 'How dare you! Fetch my tea—immediately!' Lavinia's problem meant she couldn't, or rather wouldn't make eye contact with the working classes, whereas Pimms delighted in staring at the snobbish wannabe aristocrat. Pimms wanted to wink at the woman, poke out her tongue but instead shook her head mocking Lavinia then turned and headed for the door. She spoke under her breath. 'Silly old bat.'

Lavinia heard something, knew the words were insulting but couldn't demand an explanation because the evil maid would deny anything impolite and have a plausible explanation.

As Pimms neared the door, Agatha called from the corner of the library. 'Oh Pimms, I'd like a sherry.'

Pimms stopped and smiled. 'Certainly, Madam,' said the maid.

'And pour yourself a glass,' added Agatha.

'Oh most kind, Madam,' said Pimms, grinning. 'Gawd bless you.'

With Pimms absent, Lavinia let fly although still without making eye contact with the listener. 'That woman is rude, forgetful, ignorant and frequently intoxicated.' Agatha kept working. 'Did you hear me?' She snapped. 'Agatha!'

Agatha stopped working and faced the dragon, speaking in a calm seemingly respectful voice. 'I'm sorry. Did you say something?'

'I'll have Archibald dismiss her.' Oops, that was wrong.

No longer calm and respectful, Agatha was roused to anger. Attacking the only member of her "family" was beyond the pale. She moved towards Lavinia and spoke in a stern and threatening manner.

'You'll do no such thing. Pimms has served my family forever.'

'She's a drunk!'

'*I* am responsible for staff.'

Lavinia looked at Agatha for the first time. 'Then *be* responsible instead of writing those ... ridiculous stories.'

Agatha changed personality in an instant. She pretended to be delighted as she ladled out the sarcasm. 'Mother-in-law, what can I say? You've actually *read* my humble prose? Oh, please do accept my grateful thanks.' Ah, but two could play the sarcasm game.

Lavinia grew up in Victorian times. The rules of society and the class system in vogue during the long-serving monarch's time were the rules Lavinia clung to decades later. What she said reflected her age with a liberal dash of snobbery thrown in for good measure. 'A wife should manage her household and care for her husband.'

Agatha fired back. 'Oh, of course, you mean the needlepoint and flower arranging.' Lavinia's hatred was now white hot. 'Well I'm sorry *Missus* Walloman, but I happen to enjoy creating murder mysteries.'

'And using your former married name is a slur upon my son.'

'But as Agatha Crispie, I can never sully his or your good name. After all, as you have so often said, I do write *ridiculous* stories.'

Before Lavinia could scream her reply, the bell for the end of round 1 sounded when the door opened and Elvira made her usual dramatic entrance. She would have been a natural as a silent film actress with her flamboyant gestures, exaggerated sighs and pretentious over-the-top fainting spells.

She closed the door and demanded. 'Where is my mail?'

Agatha despaired. She was already at war with Lavinia with Elvira fast becoming a second formidable foe. Agatha resumed her writing.

Lavinia held out a hand. 'Elvira! Dear child.'

Elvira moved to her grandmother. 'Good morning Grandmother.'

Agatha prepared for battle.

Chapter 7

NATURAL ALLIES, LAVINIA AND ELVIRA were united in their snobbery, their feelings of superiority, and in their mutual hated of the "foreigners"—the divorcee and her bit of baggage, Pimms.

When Lavinia and Elvira spoke to one another, they did so with raised voices to ensure Agatha caught their every word. The snobs gushed and luxuriated in the self-belief of their exceptional status.

Elvira gave her grandmother a sterile kiss then fluttered to the settee. 'How nice to see at least one person who bothers to dress in this house,' said Lavinia.

Constantly self-centred, Elvira's news was naturally about herself. 'I am expecting a super important stiffie.'

Her grandmother sighed. 'Oh an invitation; and from whom?'

Elvira sounded offended. 'How do I know without my mail?'

From her distant writing-desk, Agatha spoke without turning around. 'Pimms will have your mail.'

Agatha's comment united the others. They made faces. Lavinia was prepared to only look at people of the same class as her, and spoke to Elvira referring to Agatha in the third person.

'She's writing her latest novel, don't you know.'

Elvira caught the mocking tone. 'Really? How absolutely thrilling.'

Lavinia loved rubbing it in. 'Of course *real* writers are actually published.'

Their spite stopped when noises were heard in the hallway. The door opened and Pimms entered pushing the tea trolley. Graceful, her movements were not. Pimms stopped the trolley behind the two snobs and fussed. She made a good job of fussing.

'Now it's tea for the *old* Missus Walloman.'

Lavinia slipped back into her infuriated mood. Not only did the maid make personal comments, a sackable offence in Lavinia's world, but the word used was *old*. The fact it was accurate rubbed salt in the matriarch's wound. She retaliated.

'Coffee,' she snapped.

Pimms kept fussing and muttering then stopped. She looked at the dragon and gave her a mouthful. 'Coffee!? You said tea.'

Elvira exploded but Lavinia beat her to it. 'How dare you correct me! How dare you even speak unless spoken to. Fetch my coffee!'

Elvira joined the chorus. 'And mine! Now!'

Pimms looked from one to the other, shook her head and, while muttering, put the tea back on the trolley making a fuss. She was getting brave now. It had been more or less open warfare since day one, and Pimms was sick of being treated with contempt. As she pushed the trolley back to the door, she spoke in a quiet but audible voice.

'They say it runs in the family.'

The Wallomans looked at one another and fed off each other's fury. At the door, Pimms stopped the trolley, collected a glass of sherry and took it to Agatha.

'Your sherry, Madam.'

Agatha put down her pen. 'How kind,' she said and sipped. Pimms stepped back ready to depart when Agatha stopped her. 'Oh Pimms. I'm having trouble with the poison.'

'Poison, Madam?' enquired Pimms.

Lavinia cleared her throat which should have been enough to send the domestic on her way but no; she defied the dowager and carried on chatting with her mistress.

'I had weed killer, Pimms but I think it's a bit obvious. Any ideas?'

Elvira made a public announcement. 'We're waiting for our coffee.'

Agatha switched conversations and listeners in a flash. 'Coffee? Oh I distinctly remember your grandmother ordering tea.'

Lavinia fired back. 'Well I've changed my mind. It is permitted I presume.'

Agatha hopped up and ran with the flow. 'Of course it's permitted. I'm always changing my mind when writing mysteries; new victim, different suspect, alternative ending.'

Elvira's frustration bubbled. 'Look, I'm waiting for my mail.'

'Indeed you are,' said Agatha who turned to Pimms. 'When you return with the coffee, Pimms, kindly bring Miss Walloman's mail.'

Pimms caught the mock subservient theme. She bowed. 'Certainly Madam; coffee and correspondence it is.'

The trolley moved but stopped when Agatha raised her glass. 'Oh and Pimms, this is excellent sherry.'

'Thank you, Madam,' said the maid and they exchanged smiles.

Lavinia and Elvira saw red. Pimms opened the door then began pushing the trolley out of the library as Archie entered. He had his nose in *The Times* and Pimms was a terrible trolley pusher at the best of times. The inevitable happened.

'Hey!' shouted Archie. 'What the devil!' They yelled together.

Pimms called as loud as the patriarch. 'Oi! Mind m' trolley!'

Archie made a fuss as if he'd been hit by a truck. 'Good lord, man, watch where you're going.' He straightened his tie and newspaper, plonked himself in his favourite chair and muttered. 'Fellow's not safe in his own home.' His mother and daughter were incensed.

Pimms checked the trolley for any breakages then pushed off muttering. 'Yes Constable, he was drunk in charge of a newspaper.'

Lavinia wanted a word. 'Good morning, Archibald.'

He was still flustered. 'What? Oh, yes. Good morning, Mother.' Pimms was almost out of the library but stopped when addressed albeit incorrectly—again. 'And Timms, I'd like tea.'

Pimms found joy. Her original order could now be filled. She fussed with the brew she recently offered Lavinia. 'Lovely, I have a pot right here.'

Lavinia oozed contempt and made a demand. '*Fresh* tea.'

Pimms froze holding the pot of freshly brewed tea. Everyone sat still; on edge. Pimms sneaked a look at Agatha who gave a tiny shrug. Pimms replaced the pot and headed off mimicking Lavinia as she slipped through the door. The maid should have been on the stage.

'*Fresh* tea,' she said mimicking Lavinia. The door closed and the fury began with Elvira first out of the starting gate.

'Father, you must remove that unbearable creature.'

Lavinia joined in. 'Now, immediately.'

Archie came under attack. 'Yes, all right.' He dropped his volume. 'The problem is she came with ...' He nodded towards Agatha. '... you know who. She's part of the furniture.'

Lavinia stated a simple fact. 'You change furniture.'

Whenever Archie found himself trapped, his best tactic was to change the subject. He tried again. 'Blast! There's nothing about me in the paper.'

'She can't even fetch the mail,' bemoaned Elvira.

Archie's brain went click. Now he remembered. 'What?' he asked.

'That peasant of a maid has forgotten my mail *again*,' spat Elvira.

Archie went into defence mode, and reached inside his jacket pocket. 'Ah, mail,' he said offering up an envelope. 'There is a letter for you, Elvira. It looks like a stiffie.'

His daughter could not contain her anger. She was expecting a vitally important invitation. Each day she checked for news. The pressure mounted. The hopeless, helpless maid had been sent to finally fetch Elvira's precious post while her ignoramus of a father had the jolly thing all along. She steamed towards him and his outstretched hand holding the letter.

'Oh really,' she said. 'There is absolutely no etiquette or decorum in this house.' She snatched the envelope. 'No manners!'

Archie resumed reading his paper as his daughter sat, opened the envelope and withdrew its contents. Lavinia watched with interest while Agatha stopped her novel writing. She called from her desk.

'Is there any mail for me, dear?' Archie ignored her, his head buried in the paper. She called again. 'Archie?'

Not another interruption. He dropped his paper in annoyance. 'What now?'

'Do you have any mail for me, please?' she asked.

He remembered. 'Ah yes,' he said retrieving something again from his jacket pocket. Agatha hopped up and moved to accept her letter.

Archie read aloud the details on the envelope. 'It's from one of those London publishers—The Headley Bod.'

Agatha was annoyed. She regarded Archie's behaviour as rude, condescending and an invasion of privacy, and she was correct.

He agreed she could have her writing hobby so long as it didn't interfere with her duties as the lady of the house. More on that later.

As Agatha arrived at Archie's chair, he transferred her envelope to his other hand as if in a game of Keepings Off.

'Now, Agatha, about this writing nonsense.'

Agatha stewed. She held out a hand. 'My letter, if you please.'

'We agreed these make believe murder mysteries were not to interfere with menu-planning and flower-arranging. Yes?'

Agatha was about to politely but firmly state her case when interrupted by a loud cry. Elvira shrieked.

'Eeek! Oh my sainted aunt!' she cried.

Her father and grandmother were genuinely concerned, especially Lavinia. 'Elvira? What is it, my child?'

Elvira found it hard to breathe. Even her father caught the emotion. 'Countess Kossaroff!' she gasped.

The others all responded as one. 'Countess Kossaroff!'

Elvira was all a quiver. 'She's sent me an invitation. Me!'

Lavinia was thrilled. 'Oh at last, a social triumph.'

Even Archie caught the mood. 'I say; the aristocracy. Good show old girl!'

Elvira thought of the possibilities. 'Countess Kossaroff features in all the best magazines. She has contacts with all the right people, even at ... the Palace!'

Her family was over the moon and even Agatha found herself being caught up in the moment. 'The Palace!' echoed all three.

This was a breakthrough moment for Elvira. She'd come close to breaking into the top echelon of polite society but the important invitation never arrived—until now. Now her triumphant debut looked certain. She gushed.

'Last year, at the Savoy, I danced with a chap who danced with a girl who danced with the Prince of Sardinia.'

'Oh, how jolly super,' said her proud father.

'Now this,' beamed the breathless Elvira waving her letter.

Lavinia saw nothing but heady days ahead. 'How absolutely marvellous,' she trilled.

The family basked in the glow of Elvira's social triumph. Not so Agatha who, while impressed, failed to see the true extent of the invitation. She made a sincere comment.

'I'm sorry, I don't see the connection.'

Oh dear, wrong, wrong, wrong, Agatha. Archie, Lavinia and Elvira looked askance at Agatha unsure whether it was her ignorance or stupidity which disturbed them more. Was she jealous? Did she not want her stepdaughter to triumph in the real world with only the right people? Elvira took it upon herself to explain the facts to her uninformed stepmother.

'Oh please, Stepmother! Countess Kossaroff's good friend, Lady Eileen Bumble, organised the hunt ball last year, and her son rides to hounds with an old Etonian whose good friend knows the brother of the cousin of the neighbour of the chum of the parson of the banker of the captain of the club of that chap I danced with at the Savoy. There's the connection. I mean, what could be simpler than that?'

The others stared at Agatha. She paused then agreed she'd missed the point. 'Of course, how silly of me,' she said. Then she switched subjects and addressed her husband. 'Now Archibald, may I have my letter, if you please?' He passed it to her, forgot her, and joined in the Walloman discussion about Elvira's fabulous good fortune.

Agatha took her letter back to the writing desk and read its contents. The others continued chatting excitedly about Elvira's news. She began to announce her list of demands.

'I'll need a new gown, Father; chic, unique and expensive.'

'Naturally,' said Archie thinking money but not wanting to be branded a cheapskate when it came to his only child.

'And I simply must travel in a lavish, new motor vehicle. Are you listening, Father?'

'Of course,' added Archie mentally calculating the ever-increasing cost of his daughter's entry into polite society.

Lavinia thrilled to the possibilities. 'Your debut, my dear, will be in all the right papers; *The Times* and *The Telegraph*. Let's hope they spell your name correctly. I want all my friends in London to know I still have considerable influence in all the right circles.'

The trio's celebration slowed for a moment when they realised the other person in the room was not a party to their happiness. As one, they turned and looked at Agatha who sat at her desk reading her letter. She sensed the silence, looked up and saw all three looking at her. She pretended to be interested and spoke.

'Countess Kossaroff you say?'

Archie wanted to know about his wife's correspondence. 'By any chance, Agatha, is your letter from a publisher? I mean I don't suppose there's the remotest possibility you might have received even the hint of an offer?'

Agatha took offence. She folded the letter placing it inside the envelope. 'That's *my* business, thank you Archibald.'

The others looked at one another and smirked. *Ooooh, who's a Miss Snooty Britches?* They believed they had Agatha on the run.

Lavinia loved dealing in sarcasm. 'It couldn't possibly be another rejection of your perfect prose, I suppose.' She enjoyed her wee rhyme.

Agatha looked at them. They were all gunning for her, wishing her bad luck, wanting her to fail. Rather than stay and be humiliated, she stood and tidied her desk. She always removed her current writing project and this time, her new letter as well.

'It's a private matter. Now if you'll excuse me.'

She walked to the door making a dignified but brisk exit.

The others grinned or smirked or both.

Chapter 8

ALL THREE OF THEM WATCHED HER. The moment the door closed, the women attacked, with Lavinia going first.

'Archibald, your wife is a laughing-stock.'

'Father, she could ruin my social life; not damage, ruin.'

'I know,' said Archie.

'Her pathetic attempts at writing will damage *our* reputation.'

'My stupid stepmother is a joke.'

Archie agreed. 'Yes, yes I know, it's affecting me too. She's supposed to accompany me to social and business events but instead, she's off, God knows where, researching her latest novel.'

Lavinia went for the kill. 'And that maid of hers is beyond belief.'

Elvira was sincere. 'Did she receive an early release from prison?'

Before Archie could respond, they heard a knock on the door. He called. 'Wait!'

Elvira was on a roll. 'How can I have gentlemen calling with my stupid stepmother and her moronic maid on the loose? My marriage prospects will be cancelled; *permanently!* Did you hear me?'

The person outside in the hallway knocked again.

Archie's temper revved its engine ready for a loud getaway. He roared at the door knocker. 'I told you to wait!'

'You simply must *do* something, Father.'

'Something drastic,' added Lavinia, 'and the sooner the better.'

Archie was annoyed. Annoyed at being picked on by his family, and annoyed his wife was not keeping her end of the bargain; namely that she could enjoy a life of luxury in a country house, and potter around

52

with her novel writing on condition she perform her duties as lady of the house, and turned up at all of Archie's social and business events where he needed and wanted a wife by his side.

'Yes, all right,' he snapped at his family. 'Stop telling me what I already know.'

Lavinia went for the kill. 'You should have stopped her ridiculous writing the moment she arrived.'

Elvira went even further. 'She should never have arrived.'

'I agree,' spat Lavinia.

'Let's face it, Father; you should never have married her.'

Lavinia agreed and Archie reckoned the comments were over the top or below the belt or both.

'Enough!' he fired back. 'Elvira, you're going it a bit strong.'

'I totally agree with Elvira,' added Lavinia as if slapping her son in the face.

'Mother!' he exclaimed. Of course he knew their feelings towards Agatha but felt a gentleman's agreement should be to say nothing, and leave him to deal with his wife's peculiarities. Clearly his family had no interest in any gentleman's agreement.

Lavinia was like a dog with a bone. 'Well, are you master in your own home?' He didn't reply. 'Archie?'

He lost it and protested. 'Of course I am.'

Lavinia matched her son for volume and defiance. 'Then prove it. Stop Agatha Crispie's pathetic writing, and make her take charge of dinners and daffodils.'

Elvira threw in an addition. 'And sack the appalling Pimms.'

Archie surrendered. 'Yes, all right. You've made your point.

'Points,' said the women as one.

Lavinia reached for the small bell. 'Now,' she demanded and rang the bell.

Pimms, who had been waiting outside for what she considered ages, and all because of Archie telling her to wait, opened the door in, shall we say, a pretty foul mood. The others froze and went silent as the trolley and its driver entered and came to rest.

The maid was about to perform her duty when, puffing out his chest and trying to act as Lord of the Manor, Archie fired his order.

'Ah, Simms. Where's my coffee?'

Oh dear, Archie blew it from the off. Pimms was annoyed full stop, annoyed at the pompous Walloman family, annoyed she had to go out and come in again, and doubly annoyed at being made to stand in the hallway with the tea and coffee getting cold. So when Archie changed his order, boy, did that set the maid off in a fury?

'Coffee?' she whined. 'You ordered tea.'

Lavinia looked like she would have a heart attack. 'And she dares to correct her employer.'

Archie was not cut out to be an ogre. 'Well somebody ordered coffee.'

Elvira threw in her sarcasm. 'Oh it's here is it? Finally.'

Lavinia almost made eye contact with the lower classes. 'Serve it,' she ordered.

Pimms stood her ground. 'I can't.'

Lavinia's blood pressure soared as she impersonated Lady Bracknell upon hearing of a handbag. 'Can't?'

Pimms had no fear of her employers and certainly not by the matriarch's confected histrionics. 'Yes, you see it's gone cold.'

The three Wallomans declared in unison. 'Cold!?'

'It's gone cold because I was kept waiting outside in the hallway when some geezer shouted.' She gave a brilliant imitation of Archie's accent, volume and inflection. 'Wait! I told you to wait!'

The impersonation was so accurate it shocked the trio into silence. Suffering from apoplexy, Archie spoke first. 'Some geezer?!'

Pimms didn't wait around. The beverages were cold, and while the Wallomans struggled to contain their incandescent rage, Pimms pushed the trolley back the way she came.

'You lot wanna make up y'mind,' she said en route to the door.

Oh my. So much for being sacked as requested by Lavinia. The behaviour of the lowly maid, so blatant, so accurate and so disrespectful, knocked the trio into silence. Pimms and trolley were gone before anyone could speak. When they did, Lavinia went first.

'The unmitigated gall of the woman.'

Elvira became emotional. Real tears appeared, well, real crocodile tears. She stood and moved away to perform her dying swan routine, lost in a phoney world of despair.

'Imagine a gentleman caller even catching sight of that ... that creature. If Countess Kossaroff knew my position, I'd be ruined.' She faced her relatives. 'Do you hear? *Ruined!*'

She fled in a flood of tears slamming the door so hard, the portrait of her mother shifted on the wall. Archie stood in shock.

His mother blasted him again. 'I told you the woman's useless.'

Archie went on the defensive. 'But I never met the maid before the marriage.'

'Not Pimms, Agatha! The woman who claims to be your wife and a writer and is hopeless at both.'

Archie struggled to regain any normality. 'Yes, all right, Mother.'

'I left my home in Belgravia, and for what? My friends are in London. I could never invite them here. I'm criticised by your insensitive and talentless wife, and I can't even obtain a decent cup of tea.'

'But I thought you ordered coffee.'

Sadly, the pressure of the situation brought out the best in Archie's Mr Thicky skills. His mother exploded. 'Who cares? The point is my life here is a complete disaster.'

'Mother, please, I'll take care of Simms.'

It was all too much for Lavinia. She thumped her stick on the floor and yelled. 'It's Pimms! Her name is *Pimms!*'

Lavinia's words were loud and clear and moments later the door opened and a puffing and indignant maid appeared.

'What is it *this* time?' she protested. 'You order me out then call me back. Why don't you make up your bloomin' mind?'

Lavinia turned on Pimms, making eye-contact with a working-class person for the first time in Lavinia's 84 years. 'How dare you enter without permission?'

Pimms objected and returned serve with interest. 'You called me, Madam. "Pimms" you roared.' She imitated Lavinia and again was spot on with her mimicry. 'Pimms!'

Lavinia couldn't win. She looked away but waved at her son. 'Oh this is too much. Archibald, do something.'

'Now see here, Pimms.' He paused wondering if he had called her by the right name. 'Where's my coffee?'

'I was bringing y'tea when the senior Mrs Walloman here starts bellowing.' Lavinia seethed. 'Oh and Mrs Beeton asked me to tell you there's still a problem with that mouse in the kitchen.'

Archie lost it. 'Will you forget that damn moose and fetch my coffee?' He meant mouse but Pimms had that effect on most people.

She shook her head and spoke with emphasis. 'You're having tea.' She set off and as she neared the door, spoke frighteningly loud enough for all to hear. 'The coffee's for the battle-axe.'

The door closed. Lavinia's rage was so intense she glowed, and, had it been night, she could have read using her own light. Archie tried to regain his authority. 'That woman has got to go,' he said.

Lavinia struggled to maintain any sense of normality. 'At last. Praise be! Now imitate a man for once.' She stood and headed for the door describing her little boy as she walked. 'As a child, Archibald, you were painfully slow. Not the brightest.'

What could the poor man say? He was humiliated by his own Mama. She reached the door, paused and then tapped her stick. He understood and stepped forward to open it. Without any eye-contact, she delivered her punch line.

'Do something.'

She walked out of the library leaving Archie to close the door and reflect on what had happened in this room in the last twenty minutes. His mother, daughter and maid treated him with little or no respect. His second wife ignored his request to partner him to social events. There must be changes. But what? He decided. It was time to exert his authority starting with Agatha. After all, trying to rule his mother and daughter was undoubtedly a bridge too far.

He positioned himself beside Agatha's desk and rehearsed a speech he would deliver as soon as the opportunity allowed.

'Agatha, I've made several important decisions. No, be quiet. You will do exactly as I say. First, the grossly incompetent Pimms must go.' Anticipating her objection, he held up a hand to stop her. 'No! Wait! There's more. I haven't finished.' He paused. 'Thank you.'

He enjoyed this role playing. He felt encouraged. He moved with purpose towards the French windows and looked out over the greenest of lush lawns. 'This writing charade must stop, Agatha— now. Do you hear me?'

His confidence soared but as he rehearsed he failed to notice Pimms enter, pushing her trolley. She quietly closed the door and moved into the library. Archie let rip taking control of the game in which he had no opponent.

'Now see here, Agatha, I am a prominent businessman who is fast becoming a laughing-stock over your childish attempts at becoming another ... June Austen.'

Pimms kept fiddling with the tea caddy and spoke without lifting her head. '*Jane* Austen.'

Archie spun around furious at being spied upon and interrupted. 'How dare you interrupt?'

Pimms had his measure. She was all smiles as she lifted the pot. 'Shall I be mother, guv'nor?'

Archie huffed and puffed. 'Just pour the damn thing and go.'

He stormed out through the French windows and disappeared into the garden. The fresh air wafted inside bringing with it the sounds of nature. Birdsong from an English country garden brought a unique tranquillity to the room.

Pimms put down the teapot and crept towards the French windows, checking to see if Archie was gone. Satisfied, she moved to the large bookcase and ran her hand along the books. She stopped at her favourite tome. She knew nothing of Charles Darwin's thoughts and theories but the edition in the Walloman library of his *On the Origin of Species by Means of Natural Selection* was 500 plus pages and thus as wide as a flask, and scientific enough to never be disturbed by any of the present-day Wallomans.

She took another peek to see if anyone was around then removed the book and the flask behind it. She took a quick swig, then another. Archie appeared without warning and she panicked.

Facing the bookcase, she held the flask against her chest, breathing faster. He closed the French windows, turned and saw Pimms.

'I told you to get out,' he snapped, annoyed.

She carefully placed the flask in its hiding place and added the book. 'I was returning a book, sir.' She half smiled and then made her exit, muttering as she left. 'It was a book on spirits.'

'Out!' demanded Archie not trusting the woman, and believing her to be an agent of a foreign power, viz his wife.

At the door, she turned and added. 'On Scottish spirits actually, and your trolley's on the tea!' She didn't mean to utter a Spoonerism but, being under pressure, it just slipped out. She closed the door although could still hear the patriarch calling.

'And I don't want to be disturbed.'

She opened the door and called back. 'Very good, sir.' She paused and then poked her head back inside the room. 'So shall I tell the reporter you're not at home?'

She was clever our maid. She threw the gent a snippet of fascinating news, a teaser, and then ran away to hide. His mind exploded. The idea of a member of the Fourth Estate being on his property let alone inside his home needed time and intelligence to absorb. He hurried to the door gasping, 'Reporter?' His voice picked up decibels en route. 'Pimms! Wait!' His volume levels hit new heights. *'Pimms!'*

He yanked open the door ready to yell again but stopped as if shot. There stood the cheeky domestic with butter refusing to melt in her mouth. 'You roared, sir?'

Archie "helped" her into the library, reasonably carefully, closed the door, and gave her the third degree. He was easy to trick, was Archie, although this was no game. Or was it? 'What reporter?' he asked, or rather demanded. 'Tell me.'

Full of faux innocence and insincere bonhomie, Pimms tried to help. 'Should you have said "which reporter", sir?' she asked.

It was the last straw; grammar lessons from the char!

Chapter 9

PIMMS LOVED BEING IN CHARGE. She could easily have been on the stage. Her ability to pretend was first class, and she could use a pause to great effect. Archie desperately wanted the visitor's details.

'She arrived a few minutes ago, sir, wanting to interview the tycoon what runs the huge quarry in Cornwall.'

Archie had a thrill transplant. His toes tingled. His breath came in short pants and even his short pants were excited. Being successful in business was essential but having the world told of his success was the key to his happiness. A reporter meant publicity. He bubbled.

'But that's me. *I'm* the tycoon. She's come to interview me!' He turned away from the unimportant and dwelt on uplifting thoughts. 'At last, I've been discovered; recognition and fame are surely mine.'

'She said her name was Miss Dorothy S. Layers and she works for the media baron, Lord Peter Fancy.'

Archie's eyes sparkled, his heart raced and he developed a twitch. 'I say!' He returned to planet Earth and addressed Pimms. 'Well show her in, man. Show her in.'

'Right you are, sir,' said Pimms, heading off to find the reporter.

Archie called and Pimms stopped at the door. 'And I'm not to be disturbed by anyone. Have you got that?'

'Not even by your wife, sir?'

'*Especially* not by my wife.' He spoke emphatically. 'Keep her out!'

Pimms tapped her nose with her finger. 'No visitors it is, *sir.*'

She departed and closed the door. Archie slipped into a panic. He looked around then plumped a cushion or three, talking as he did so.

'Keep calm, Archie. You're the tycoon. You're in charge. Here's your chance to impress.'

He froze when a door knock sounded. He fiddled with his tie, patted his hair and moved away from the door. Mr Pompous spoke.

'En*ter*,' he said with the second syllable going free range.

Nothing happened and Archie worried. He cleared his throat ready for a second command when the door opened and Pimms bowled in, stopped beside Archie and curtsied. He didn't know if this was a prank or he'd been listed in the King's New Year's Honours' List. Dream on, Arch.

Pimms must have thought he had because she spoke with an awfully hoity-toity accent of which Lavinia would have been proud.

'Miss Dorothy S. Layers,' she announced making a sweeping gesture towards the hallway. Archie was struck dumb and frozen to the spot. His jaw dropped and stayed there. Nothing happened and then this woman bowled in straight from a game of hockey with the gels in the Upper Fifth.

She had teeth to make a horse jealous, the brightest wig with more curls than a surf beach, and glasses so thick they made her and especially her eyes sea-sick. She had a permanent squint.

Pimms twigged and left. At the door, she looked back at Archie and tapped her nose. She mouthed the words, "No wife" and left closing the door. Archie didn't notice Pimms, being too busy with the galloping octopus in his library.

Clasping a giant notepad and equally large pencil in one hand, she extended her other hand and spoke.

'Mr Walloman, how awfully kind of you to see me,' she said giving a hyperventilating laugh which might have been a whinny from a horse. In fact Archie momentarily thought she'd tethered her animal on the lawn.

As they shook hands, Archie tried to turn on the charm. 'It's lovely to meet you ...'

'Miss Layers,' she helped him out.

'Miss Layers,' he said nodding and smiling simultaneously. 'I'm always delighted to assist members of the press, especially one so utterly charming.'

Her took her hand and kissed it prompting her to again borrow her laugh from the stables at Epsom.

'When I was asked to interview you, I thought it was one of Lord Peter's whimsies.' The laugh popped out again after which she took in the surrounds. 'Oh what a delightful room,' she said now adding a *w* to words with an *r* making the last comment, a delightful womb.

'Thank you,' said Archie. He indicated the settee. 'Shall we begin?'

She sat but appeared secretive and serious then whispered. 'First, sir, I have a question about secoowity.'

Archie caught her mood and whispered in reply. 'Secoowity?'

Dorothy put a finger to her lips. 'Shhh.'

Archie was hooked. 'I say, are we in any danger?'

She patted the settee and Archie felt compelled to sit beside her— but not too close.

'You must know, sir, newspaper bawons gweatly admire you; a bwilliant businessman and entwepreneur.'

Archie luxuriated in the flattery. 'Well naturally I know that but one never likes to blow one's own trumpet.' Oh yes, one does.

'Your opinions are highly wegarded, sir, which natuwally leads to the possibility of spies.'

'Spies?' gasped Archie, in shock. 'Really? I mean, Weally?'

'Most definitely which is why I would like to request you close the curtains wight now.'

'What?' exclaimed a startled Archie. This was an extraordinary request. *Imagine what Mother would say.* 'You want me to close the curtains?'

'But turn on the lights of course.'

Archie felt relieved but excited. 'Of course.' He stood and moved to the French windows. 'Allow me.' He began to close the curtains.

She stood. 'I can turn on the lights. Where is the switch, please?'

'It's on the wall by the door.' He pointed as he closed the curtains.

'Jolly good,' said Dorothy, giving a little horsey laugh. She went to the wall switch and turned on the lights as Archie closed the last of the curtains. The room was lit and she returned to the settee and prepared her oversized notepad and pencil.

Archie remembered his manners. 'Oh I say, can I offer you a drink, Miss ... er ...'

'Layers.'

'Miss Layers?'

She declined his offer and launched into the interview. 'Now, sir, about your latest mining venture in Cornwall; a little bird tells me the survey wesults are most pwomising.'

Archie did a double take. 'How did you know about the survey? It's meant to be top secret. It *is* top secret.'

'Oh come now, Mr Walloman, what did I did tell you about spies?'

Archie was now a true believer. 'You did. Gosh I didn't think it was true.'

'So tell me about this new venture of yours?'

Archie loved talking about himself. 'Oh it'll certainly be another of my spectacular successes.'

Dorothy spoke as she wrote. 'Spec ... tac ... u ... lar ... suc ... cesses.' He beamed. 'And what of your future plans?'

'Oh the usual; I'll make the shareholders a small fortune.'

She scribbled again. 'Share ... holders ... fortune.' She smiled at him. 'Gosh, this *is* a scoop.'

Archie looked puzzled. 'You know, there is something about your appearance, Miss Layers, I can't quite pick. Have we met before?'

'Oh I don't think so. I would certainly wemember such a successful entwepweneur as your good self.'

Archie lapped it up. 'True, true and you know something; I've never been interviewed by a female reporter.' He moved slightly to sit a little bit closer. 'And certainly not by one so attwactive.'

She re-arranged her position moving subtly away from Archie. 'So tell me, Mr Walloman, now that women have the wight to vote, what is your opinion on the subject of women having a caweer?'

'Oh I'm absolutely in favour. Why, my wife has a caweer. She's the well-known mystewy witer Agatha Cwispie.'

'Really? I mean weally? I don't think I've heard of her. Tell me, what are the titles of her most successful books?'

Archie floundered in a mess of his own making. 'Oh, ah, let me think. There's the ...' Of course he had no idea.

'One will do. What's your favouwite book witten by Agatha Cwispie?'

'Gosh, it's on the tip of my tongue. It's … No, no it's gone.' He saw a chance to change subjects. 'You see I'm more a *Times* and *Telegraph* tycoon, which means I could weally help your caweer, young lady.'

Dorothy rose and took in the room. 'I do so love this libwary. You have exquisite taste.' Archie lapped it up. 'It's quite ware in a man.'

Archie's false modesty bordered on pathetic. 'One does one's best.'

She placed her notepad and pencil on a cabinet and admired a painting on the wall by the door. 'This painting is so beautiful.' She turned and looked at the opposite wall and pointed. 'And so is that.'

Archie turned to see which painting she meant. The lights went out and a choked scream was heard. He swore.

'Damn, a fuse must have blown.' He set off in the darkened room towards the light switch. 'Stay where you are, Miss Layers. I'll have this fixed in a jiffy.'

He reached the wall and felt for the switch in the dark. 'How strange,' he said. 'The switch is turned off. Never mind, here we go.'

He flicked the switch and the room filled with light. He turned to address his visitor and nearly died.

'Miss Layers,' he gasped and ran to the settee. Once there, he screamed. 'Miss Layers!'

No wonder he panicked. Miss Layers lay on her back on the settee, motionless, with one hand clutching the top of a knife with its blade firmly inserted, up to the hilt, in her chest.

Archie stood behind the settee bending over seeking to help the unfortunate woman. 'My God, what's happened?' He moved closer, trembling. 'Are you not well, Miss? Where did you find that knife?' He stopped addressing her and moved towards the door and shouted. 'Help! Somebody help!' He hurried back to the reclining reporter.

'Come along, Miss, there's no need for this. We haven't finished the interview. You haven't asked about my golf handicap.' Again he shouted at the door. 'Help! Will somebody please help me!'

Pimms opened the door and noticed the curtains were closed and the lights on. 'Oi, what's goin' on in here?'

He beckoned wildly. 'Come here, come here, and close the door.'

Pimms closed the door. 'I thought you said no interruptions.'

Archie was a mixture of trembling, perspiring and wanting to pee. 'Will you please come here,' he demanded. 'There is something not absolutely pukka about our visitor.'

Pimms stood beside Archie and looked at Miss Layers. 'I think you might be right, sir. Do people normally keep a knife in their chest?'

'What?'

'I've never seen a person store one in that position.'

He nodded. 'I agree, it does look a tad awkward,' said a terrified Archie.

'And what's the stocking doing around her throat?' asked Pimms.

'I have no idea. Do you think it might be the latest fashion?' garbled a desperate Archie.

'Funny about the clothes-peg on her nose though,' noted Pimms.

'Why? What's funny about it?'

'And there's a pocket full of rye spilling out of her mouth.'

'Too much whisky?' asked a despairing Archie.

Pimms looked at him. 'What, you, me or her?'

Archie was dying. 'Oh my lord, what's it all mean?'

'I think it means she's dead, sir.'

Shock smashed Archie. 'Dead? She can't be. Are you sure?'

'Well,' said Pimms, 'if she's alive, strong liquor has never passed my lips.'

Archie despaired. 'We were discussing my career when the lights went out and ... Oh no!'

'What?' asked a genuinely interested Pimms. Archie struggled to say the dreaded words. With terror in his voice, he gasped.

'There's a body in the library!'

Chapter 10

PIMMS HAD SEEN A LOT in her life and this body in the library business was nothing special. You see, Agatha's grandmother entertained some pretty weird visitors over the years, and being from Yorkshire, Pimms well understood the saying, "There's nowt so queer as folk". So the corpse on the couch didn't rattle the maid. And she loved being able to give Mr Walloman a really tough time.

'I shouldn't worry, sir,' said Pimms. 'She's only a reporter.'

Archie hit the panic button. He nearly collapsed and leant on the settee to stop fainting. 'Only! Are you mad? This means scandal. I'll be ruined.' He turned to Pimms and pleaded. 'What'll I do? Help me.' He begged. 'Please, help me!'

'Brandy's what we need, sir.' She headed to the liquor cabinet. 'Doubles all round I say,' but stopped when Archie called.

He'd solved the problem. 'I know; heart attack.'

Pimms moved back to Archie and the body in the library. She was playing him on a string. 'But you don't even look sick, sir.'

Archie snapped. 'What? No! Not me; her!' He pointed at the body.

'Well so would you, sir, with a knife stuck in your chest.'

'We need a doctor.' He headed to Agatha's writing desk. 'Agatha has a list of doctors in her mysteries.' He fiddled and found the list.

'Those mysteries are fiction, sir,' called Pimms. 'They're not real.'

He wasn't listening and looked. 'I'll call ah, Doctor Thompson.'

He turned to Pimms for confirmation. She knew all the characters in Agatha's books and shook her head. 'Sorry, sir; but he's a doctor of archaeology.'

'Damn.' He looked again. 'Well then I'll call ... Doctor Pender.'

'No use, sir. He's a clergyman.'

'Blast,' muttered Archie and continued searching. 'Well here's one—Doctor Llewellyn Knox.' He set off. 'I'll send for Doctor Knox.' He opened the door and yelled back to Pimms. 'Open the lights and turn on the curtains.' He fled.

Pimms shook her head and started to open the curtains. At the French windows with her back to Miss Layers still motionless and stretched out on the settee, Pimms spoke to herself.

'I shouldn't bother, sir. Doctor Knox is an evangelist.'

Then Pimms heard an eerie voice. It was ghost-like and its sound and message fairly put the wind up the normally unflappable maid. 'Who raises people from the dead.'

Pimms froze. The words were scary but the sound of the voice, unusual and weird, genuinely frightened the old girl. She spun around and saw no-one. Miss Layers was as stiff as a stiff.

The curtains were open with the lights still on. Pimms made a bee-line for the switch and, to keep up her spirits, she repeated her last sentence as she hurried across the room.

'I shouldn't bother, sir. Doctor Knox is an evangelist.'

Pimms finished the speech as she reached the light switch. She flicked it and the lights went off as the strange voice was heard again.

'Who raises people from the dead.'

Silence dominated the room. Pimms was breathing heavily before she heard the spooky voice the first time. After the second incantation, her breath switched to rapid. She forced herself to turn around. As she pressed back against the library door, the dead Dorothy slowly rose from a supine to a sitting position.

'Oh my godfather,' cried Pimms; 'you is alive!'

Layers stood, removed her hat, wig and glasses in one movement and tossed them on the settee. She looked at Pimms and spoke in a well-known voice.

'Of course I'm alive, Pimms; it's me,' said Agatha putting the detritus of her staged murder in the pockets of her coat.

Pimms staggered towards her genuinely shocked. 'Madam? Is it really you?'

'Don't be silly, Pimms. Of course it's me. You knew all along.'

66

'Upon my soul, Madam, I never did.'

Agatha was surprised and pleased. 'Really? Truly?'

'Yes, really and truly.'

'How fantastic. If I can fool you, I can certainly fool my readers.'

Pimms wanted to ask, "What readers?" but settled for, 'Yes, and excuse my French, Madam, but what the hell were you doing?'

'Oh come on, Pimms, what do you think? I was testing an idea for my new mystery. Did you like it?' She removed her coat.

'What I think doesn't matter, Madam. It's what will Mr Walloman think that counts.'

'Oh he'll be thrilled. He told me women should have a career.'

'But he thinks you're a dead reporter. He knows nothing about you changing your name to Lazarus.'

'And he never will so remember, Pimms, Mum's the word.'

Pimms struggled to understand what had happened in the last five minutes, and had no idea how to handle the next five.

'But I'll have to tell him something, Madam. He's just seen a female reporter murdered in his library.'

Agatha thought about it. 'Hmm, perhaps you're right.'

'I think it's a little more than perhaps, Madam.'

'Okay, I want you to invent a story.'

Pimms didn't have a clue. 'Me? Invent a story? I don't even look like Charles Dickens.'

Agatha rattled off a story line and, in the middle of the speech, slipped into a broad Scottish accent. 'Tell him a tall, dark Scotsman burst into the room, saw the body, cried out, "Och aye, I love you Mrs McGinty" and carried the body out through those French windows.'

Pimms struggled. 'I'll never remember all that, Madam.'

Clutching her props, Agatha headed to the wall of books. 'Pretend it's my best ever whodunit.' She almost threatened Pimms. 'But don't say I made it up.' She touched a hidden switch beside a particular book and a panel opened inwards. Agatha stepped through, called, 'Bye!' and disappeared with the panel closing tight behind her.

Pimms was alone, dumbfounded and distressed. 'Oh Gawd, what'll I say?' She spotted the clothes peg Agatha wore on her nose when pretending to be dead. Pimms hurried to pick it up.

'You've left the clothes peg.' She sort of called, 'Madam!'

Before she could say anymore, she heard footsteps outside the library so threw the clothes peg towards the bookshelves and turned as Archie burst in and closed the door.

He was back to breathing in short pants. 'I couldn't raise any of Agatha's doctors.' He saw the empty settee and, transfixed, moved to examine it. 'What's happened?' He looked around the library then stared at the mute maid. 'Where's the body?'

Pimms became the perfect witness for the defence. 'Which body did you have in mind, sir?'

Archie was beside himself before he left the library. Now he was beside, behind and beneath himself. 'Which body?' he gasped. 'How many are there? I mean the one stabbed, strangled and suffocated.'

Pimms remembered. 'Oh *that* body.'

'Yes, *that* body. Where the hell is it?'

Pimms had a bash at following Agatha's orders. The maid had natural acting skills but remembering lines put a real strain on her well-lubricated brain. She perfected the Scottish accent and recited all the words with a wee stumble over the geography of the windows. She raised a finger indicating her willingness to begin and let rip.

'A tall, dark Scotsman burst into the room, saw the body, cried out, "Och aye, I love you Mrs McGinty" and carried the body out through them Irish windows.'

It was so implausible it was plausible. Archie stood gobsmacked. 'Just like that?' he asked.

Pimms came to believe it herself but over-egged the pudding. 'Yes sir, just like that. It's a real who-dooed-it.'

Archie scrunched his face. 'A real who-dooed-it?'

Pimms remembered the correct term. 'Oh, forgive me, sir. I meant it's a real who*dun*it.'

Archie felt his grip on life slipping. 'This is not happening,' he said leaning on the back of the settee. 'I need a drink.'

Pimms came alive. 'Excellent idea, sir' she said heading to the liquor cabinet. 'What'll we have?'

Before a glass could be poured, the library door was flung open, and Lavinia entered in a smouldering rage. Even her walking stick was angry. Her voice became a loaded weapon. 'This is outrageous. Archibald, how could you?' She crossed to her chair, was about to sit but stopped and looked. She paused. 'Where's the body?'

Archie decided to play a stupid game of pretence which was never going to work. 'Body, Mother? Which body do you mean?'

Lavinia sat and fumed. She would never believe anything her son would say anyway. 'Is this one of your pathetic jokes?'

'It's not, Mother, and there's been a development.' He tried to remember the words of Pimms, managed the French accent well, but again failed with certain geographic details. 'A short, fair Frenchman burst into the room, cried out, "Oooooo, Madame McGinty, Je t'aime!" and carried the body out through those German windows.'

It was so unbelievable it was believable. Before Lavinia could attack her son and his ludicrous explanation, the door flew open again, and this time Elvira burst in over-acting like never before.

'I hate you, Father!' she screamed. 'This scandal means I must decline Countess Kossaroff's invitation and my only chance at becoming a genuine aristocrat. I could have married a prince.' She paused as everyone stared at her. She looked around. Her outrage softened a tad. She paused. 'Where's the body?'

'It's gone,' said her grandmother.

'Gone? Gone where? How?' demanded Elvira.

Lavinia explained getting her guttural German accent spot on but again failing the country identification bit. 'Your father believes a giant German burst into the library, cried out, "Achtung! Frau McGinty, Ich liebe dich!" and carried the body out through those Scottish windows.'

Elvira underwent a personality makeover. She was thrilled. 'But, but that's marvellous.'

The others spoke as one. 'Marvellous?'

Elvira explained. 'If there's no body, there's no murder and no murder means no scandal. Cinderella can go to the ball after all.'

'Cinderella?' asked Pimms who was ignored. She was invisible.

As Elvira sat following her over-the-top performance, Agatha appeared in the library doorway, flushed and excited. 'A body? A real body?' She entered. 'Do we have our very own murder mystery? Oh how absolutely delicious.' She stopped. The others stared at her—glared at her. She realised and changed character in a second. 'Oh, how terrible, how awful; it's such a tragic, wicked waste.'

The others went for her with venom; Lavinia first. 'A heinous crime is committed in our house, in this room and *she* is delighted.'

Agatha tried to defend her action. 'No I'm not, really, I promise.'

Elvira opened from the other end. 'A foul, unspeakable deed occurs in our home where the Wallomans have lived for hundreds of years, and *she* is amused.'

Agatha slipped into her contrite outfit. 'Oh, do please forgive me. We writers need inspiration and when I heard about a body being found in the library, I naturally thought of my work. I'm so, so sorry.'

Archie fought for control. 'This time, Agatha, we may forgive you.'

'No we won't,' snapped his mother.

'Never,' spat Elvira.

He continued. 'But you must accept it was all a misunderstanding.'

She wanted to argue. 'A misunderstanding?'

'Yes,' snapped the Wallomans.'

'Are you sure?' she queried.

'Yes,' snapped the Wallomans with even greater force.

'Of course we're sure,' snapped Archie, gaining strength, 'there *is* no body; there *was* no body and you cannot even talk about, let alone investigate a murder, if there is no body. Do you understand?'

Agatha had put far too much effort into her game, her charade, her plotting to surrender so easily, meaning she would never give up without a fight. 'But I heard you all talking about it.'

'No you didn't,' spat Lavinia.

'You're going deaf,' added Elvira. She spoke loudly. 'Hello?'

'Nothing happened,' added Archie as all three gave Agatha the stare of death. She decided to fight fire with fire.

'Oh come on, I heard you, the whole house heard you.' She looked at Archie and mimicked him. "Help! Somebody help!" you shouted. Even I heard it and I was miles away upstairs in my room,' said the fibbing would-be writer. A staring competition began. Who would blink first? Agatha looked around the room and spotted Pimms trying to hide. 'Pimms, you saw the body. Tell them.'

An unhappy Pimms hesitated. 'Well I, I, is a bit confused, Madam.'

Archie took control. 'She's confused and she's leaving.' He looked at Pimms and pointed to the door. 'You, leave now!'

Agatha called. 'Wait!' Pimms stopped. You could smell the tension. 'I want the truth, Pimms.' She turned to her maid who was now the reluctant star of the show. Many feelings, especially hatred, filled the library with most, no, with all of it directed at the maid. 'Pimms, what did you see?'

Poor old Pimms was torn between being loyal to the family she had served forever, and grassing on her current boss thereby getting Agatha into serious trouble. Would Pimms lie? No, she plumped for her boss. 'I did see a dead body,' she said. The trio exploded while Agatha grinned. 'It was there on the settee.' Pimms pointed.

Elvira, currently sitting near the spot indicated by Pimms, shifted sharpish making a face of disgust. 'Errghh,' she spluttered.

'Sack her,' snapped Lavinia pointing at Pimms.

'Shoot her,' added Elvira.

Archie cracked, the pressure being too much. 'Oh it's no use,' he wailed. 'Pimms is right. There was a dead woman, there on the settee.'

This was far too much information for Elvira who moved, standing behind her grandmother. They would support one another. Lavinia could not believe the pathetic surrender of her son.

'You spineless weakling,' she hissed. He felt even worse.

Agatha felt terrific and spoke with a calm and reasonable voice. 'Thank you, Archie. Now we need to call the police.'

Oh dear. Had Agatha cursed the King, smashed every window in the house, and stripped naked on the front lawn, her behaviour would have aroused a much smaller response than that caused by her last remark. The Wallomans erupted. Even faithful Pimms, who knew the truth of the charade with Miss Layers, joined in the shouted reaction.

'The police!'

'Are you insane?' barked Archie.

'Our class of person never calls the police,' spat Lavinia.

'Countess Kossaroff has never even *heard* of the police!' screamed Elvira.

Agatha protested. 'But there's been a murder. We cannot ignore such an event and so must call the police.'

'And say what?' demanded Archie. 'Yes officer, she was stabbed, strangled and suffocated, but now she's scarpered!'

Agatha wouldn't let it go. She wanted to write the best ever murder mystery and needed the official involvement of the law to help test her plot. 'But a missing body adds tension, it deepens the mystery,' she argued then turned to her husband. 'So, Archie, did you recognise the woman?'

'No, absolutely not.'

'But you must have noticed something. In a word, how would you describe her?'

Archie didn't need any think music. 'Plump,' he said.

Agatha was shocked, hurt or both. 'Plump?'

Archie rammed it home. 'Yes, she was plump and plain; *very* plain.'

Pimms nearly died. 'Oh Gawd!'

'Plain and plump?' asked Agatha with a feeling of anger.

'And frumpish,' added Archie with spite.

Agatha shook her head and turned to her maid. 'Pimms, would you describe our mystery woman as a plain, plump frump?'

Pimms felt the walls closing in and went all apologetic. 'I'm terribly sorry, Madam, I only saw the woman from a distance.'

'No you didn't,' argued Archie, pointing. 'You stood right there, next to the corpse.'

Lavinia snapped. 'Archibald, stop this appalling travesty.'

'Come now, Pimms,' pressed Agatha. 'The police will want to know.'

Elvira took over. 'The police will *not* want to know. They won't *be* here.'

Agatha was on a roll. 'Nonsense, of course we're having the police.'

'No police!' thundered Elvira.

'Wait,' said Archie, desperate for a peaceful resolution. 'I've thought of a way to solve the mystery without involving the police.'

'This had better be good,' warned Lavinia.

'We could ask that old biddy from the village; the one who solves mysteries.'

Agatha scoffed. 'Oh please, not the silly spinster sleuth, Miss Mary Mead.'

'But can she keep a secret? Is she a gossip?' asked Lavinia.

'We'll make her,' said Archie. 'She'll solve the mystery but tell only us. Besides, no body means no crime occurred.'

Agatha persisted. 'I still say we should call the police.'

'No police,' thundered the Walloman chorus.

'But we need a resolution. You can't have a mystery with a body in the library without a denouement.'

Elvira wanted this mess sorted. 'Send for this Mary Mead woman, give her strict instructions, and pray she isn't a gossip.'

'I agree,' said Lavinia pointing at Pimms. 'You, send for her now.'

Pimms left muttering and Elvira returned, carefully, to the settee.

The Wallomans wanted this incident solved, settled or preferably buried, and with a minimum of fuss. Agatha didn't and tried a new tack. She was desperate to have an official investigation so as to make her mystery as gripping and as real as possible. She attacked the amateur detective.

'Oh please; how is a dotty old maid going to help?'

'Because,' said Archie, 'if there's anything suspicious, she'll expose it yet we control the situation. That's the important thing; secrecy.'

Agatha continued ridiculing Miss Mead. 'She made a few lucky guesses in a few boring, straightforward murders where anyone could have picked the murderer in the first five pages. She isn't a patch on Sherlock Holmes.'

Archie responded with sarcasm. 'Sherlock Holmes?' he scoffed. 'He isn't real. He's a chap in a book. Good lord, Agatha, can't you tell the difference between fiction and real life?'

Agatha had no choice. She took a stand. 'Well I'm going to call the police.' She headed for the door but stopped when Elvira uttered a withering response.

'You do, Stepmother, and there *will* be a murder—yours!'

This produced a cliff-hanger moment. Elvira wasn't bluffing, and Agatha believed the threat, as did both Lavinia and Archie. It's a fact that if you try and come between a desperate, young, stuck-up socialite and her appearance at the social event of the year, then the socialite will do anything to protect her moment of fame. Spilling blood is nothing; it's the minimum price to pay. Elvira would happily kill to obtain her chance at stardom. So Agatha faced the challenge. Go for the police and finish up as the real body in the library, or back off. The others stared at the writer. Did she have the bottle? Before Agatha could say or do anything, Pimms burst into the room.

'How dare you enter without knocking. Get out!' roared Lavinia.

Pimms puffed. Any exertion at her age was a worry. She fought to relay her message between heavy breathing. 'Sorry, but I think there's an important event you ought to know about.'

'Have you sent for Miss Mary Mead?' demanded Archie.

'Yes, I have but ...' She needed to catch her breath. 'But there's a policeman outside.'

Chapter 11

THE LIBRARY EXPLODED. 'What!?' cried everyone including Agatha, although she was delighted while the others were confused, fearful and furious.

Elvira slumped on the settee. She had, in old-fashioned terms, a fit of the vapours. 'It's the end. My life is over,' she despaired.

Agatha was ready to start hopping on the spot. She clasped her hands to try and hide her glee. 'Is he a *real* policeman?'

Pimms delivered more pain. 'He said he was from Scotland Yard.'

Archie lost it. 'Scotland Yard! What'll we do?'

Lavinia drew on her inner strength. 'We will stay perfectly calm and send him back to Scotland.' She too was under pressure.

Pimms began to breathe normally. 'He said his name was Sir Henry Dither-something.'

'Henry Dithering!' exclaimed Archie with joy and relief.

'That's him,' said Pimms.

'Oh, show him in, show him in. Henry and I are old pals,' added a smiling Archie wiping sweat from his brow.

Pimms looked at Archie then the others, shrugged and exited mimicking Archie as she went. 'Oh, show him in, show him in.'

'Father, I warn you,' threatened Elvira.

'You're playing with fire, Archibald,' threatened Lavinia.

Archie was calmness personified. 'Relax, he's retired. I once told him to drop in if he was ever in the area. It's only a social call.'

Agatha's excitement bubbled. 'So we can ask Sir Henry about the murder?'

'No!' thundered the trio.

'There was no murder. Tell her, Father,' said Elvira, 'now!'

Archie puffed himself up to his modest height and tried to look important. 'Agatha, I forbid you to even mention the body in the library. Is that clear?'

Agatha was angry and about to challenge the order when Pimms entered and made an announcement as if she were at a high society ball announcing Lord and Lady Muck.

'Me Lords, Ladies and Gentlemen, Sir Dithering Henry.'

The others were so desperate about what the guest might look like, say or do, they ignored Pimms and her prattling pronunciation. Sir Henry had no idea.

Archie stepped forward as the guest entered. 'Henry, my dear fellow, how lovely to see you.'

The men shook hands warmly as Henry, imitating an upper-class nincompoop, gushed. 'Archie, by Jove—spiffing to see you—what?'

'You're looking remarkably well, old chap.'

'In the area—popped in—off-chance—not interrupting I hope—what?'

Lavinia and her granddaughter exchanged glances. Agatha had serious doubts about this so-called detective, and Pimms made a dash for the door and escaped. She didn't want to be called as a witness for either side.

'Of course you're not interrupting. Now, Henry, you know Mother.'

Archie indicated Lavinia but Henry never remembered a face and so made a bee-line for Agatha stunning the others. Scotland Yard's finest he wasn't and, now retired, he'd become even worse.

'Of course,' beamed Henry who took Agatha's hand and kissed it. 'Hello dear Mother—jolly good—what?'

This had not begun well; could not have been worse more like. Tension bubbled away. Will they be able to keep this loopy detective on a leash? Archie tried to right the ship.

'Ah, no Henry; you haven't met my wife.'

Henry was now on a roll and compounded his initial error. He turned to Elvira and again took her hand. 'I say—new spouse—ravishing—what?' He kissed her hand.

Elvira was terrified. If she corrected Sir Henry, would he feel embarrassed and turn nasty? She looked for help from her father.

He was all at sea making signs behind Henry's back, using mini waves, and shakes of his head, as he tried to have Elvira play along with the mistake. *Don't correct him! Say nothing! No!*

'Sir Henry,' smiled Elvira.

The visitor took over. He indicated the women he named. 'So, met Archie's mother—his lovely wife—...' He looked around and spied Lavinia. 'Which means you must be ...'

Lavinia raced to speak first and threw in her reply. 'I'm Archie's sister.'

Her claim stunned everyone, even Agatha although she, like the others had no idea how this visit would end. Her dream of a cutting police mind tackling her body in the library case was vanishing with each passing second. In short, Sir Henry was a goose.

He didn't hear Lavinia announce her new status so carried on with his guessing. 'Archie's grandmother—how do—what?'

Lavinia was poised to erupt. Archie discovered the art of the nervous laugh. 'Oh, Henry, you are a wag; always one with ladies, hey? Come and sit down old chap, over here.'

Subtle was never a word you could apply to Henry Dithering. He prattled as he sat. 'Tally ho—jolly good—top hole—I say—what!'

With Henry settled on the settee beside Elvira, and smiling at the clearly nervous young woman, Agatha wondered if her hopes might still be realized. The police were here albeit in the form of a stereotypical thick-as-two-short-planks detective. But could she test her murder mystery plot? She spoke.

'Excuse me, Sir Henry, could you clear up a little problem for me.'

'Oh absolutely I can, Mother dear.'

'Is it true all policemen have a razor-sharp mind, and a keen eye for detail?'

'True? Nothing could be *more* true. Don't you be misled by those terrible detective tales where the police are portrayed as buffoons not knowing their right elbow from their left.' Henry indicated as he spoke, and tapped his left elbow when he said *right* and naturally, his right elbow when he said *left*. The family watched with a mixture of horror and incomprehension. He may as well have been wearing a sandwich-board advertising his real name of "Mr Thicky".

Agatha pressed ahead. 'Now by detective tales, Sir Henry, do you mean murder mysteries?'

'They're the ones, exactly, where the police plod along one step behind an eccentric amateur. Oh dear,' he said shaking his head. 'Not true, not true at all.'

Agatha struggled to believe him. 'And are you sure about that, sir?'

He nodded. 'As sure as I'm standing here,' he said, sitting on the settee. 'Why today's detectives are supremely intelligent.'

Archie tried to muscle in on the conversation thinking that if he became a part of it, he might be able to control it. 'We have an amateur detective in our village, Henry,' he said, 'a Miss Mary Mead.'

'Oh charming woman,' replied Sir Henry, 'absolutely charming.' He paused, raised his eyebrows and spoke more intimately. 'But has no idea about solving mysteries, what!'

Pimms knocked and entered without being called, much to Lavinia's disgust.

Archie tried to take control. 'Yes, Pimms, what is so important you must interrupt?'

'You asked me to send for the silly old moo from the village.'

'What?' asked Archie not understanding Miss Mead's description.

'Well she's here.'

The announcement caused concern. Agatha didn't want her session with the policeman to go awry. The Walloman trio wanted the body in the library incident to remain a state secret. And Sir Henry, being as dumb as a plum, could say or do anything. However, Miss Mead was sharp, and the family knew it was a fine line between getting away with murder, and having their upper-class reputation dragged through the mud. The spinster entered.

Lavinia pretended to be pleased. Her life was one big sham and her insincerity won awards. 'Ah, Miss Mary Mead, good morning.'

The village sleuth clutched her ever-present small basket. She was dressed appropriately for a middle-aged spinster resident in a quiet village, wearing tweed and more tweed, plus a basic hat with her graying hair well under control. The soles of her sensible shoes were ironed flat. Henry and Archie rose to greet the lady.

'Miss Mead,' announced Archie. 'How kind it is of you to call.'

She was surprised at the size of the gathering. 'Oh, good morning,' she said. To match Sir Henry constantly saying "What!" she was good at saying "Oh".

Archie indicated an armchair. 'Please, do sit, Miss Mead.'

'Oh, thank you, most kind,' she said, 'thank you.'

Archie indicated his other visitor. 'Now Miss Mead, I understand you've already met this famous detective.'

She spied the grinning chap. 'Oh yes, good morning, Sir Henry.'

Henry nodded. 'Good afternoon dear lady,' he said and sat.

'I think we last worked together on a murder with a body in the library,' she said.

The Wallomans gasped. *They worked together on a murder case featuring a body in the library!? Help!*

Henry kept smiling. 'We did, we did and where, if I remember correctly, you made a very lucky guess.'

Miss Mead graciously smiled. 'You're too kind, Sir Henry.'

Now with the guests, plural, and everyone seated, the tricky question arose. No, it was more than tricky. The family had sent for Miss Mead to quietly sort out the body in the library saga with an emphasis on *quietly*. How could they do so now with ace detective Dithering in their midst? The family members were flying on a wing and a prayer.

How much small talk is okay? How can we separate the visitors?

Lavinia led the pack. 'Delightful weather we're having, Miss Mead?'

Silent sighs of relief from Archie and Elvira. Agatha remained fascinated and hopeful. Nobody noticed Pimms had moved towards Agatha's desk where she watched with eager anticipation. Pimms was in fact unique in this setting. She alone knew the identity of the murder victim and her or its current locale, and had seen the whole two acts from the front stalls.

'Indeed,' said Miss Mead. 'I was only pruning my roses this morning and I said to myself, "Isn't this delightful weather"?'

'Indeed, indeed,' added Archie who desperately tried but failed to think of any inane chatter to keep the conversation going. Pressure built in the room. Henry didn't notice the tense atmosphere—why would he?—but still managed to light the fuse attached to the barrels of gunpowder packed around and under Lavinia's chair.

He blundered in with, 'So what brings you here, Miss Mead?'

A vast amount of oxygen instantly left the library as anyone with the name of Walloman snatched a sharp yet massive intake of breath. Then followed an 8½ month pregnant pause as every eye fixed on the silly old moo from the village.

Surely she won't mention the m word?

Miss Mead didn't know the meaning of panic and spoke in her usual measured and unremarkable voice.

'Oh, the same as you, Sir Henry; murder!' Darn, she did mention the m word.

So with the fuse fizzing, a moment later the inevitable explosion followed. Lavinia and Elvira suffered extreme heart palpitations with the matriarch swearing—well, a polite form thereof—under her breath, while Archie felt inclined to cry. Elvira lost her voice. Agatha didn't know whether to cheer or curse, and Pimms took huge delight in seeing the horrible family members suffer.

Sir Henry joined the Walloman chorus. 'Murder?!' they exclaimed.

Miss Mead reacted but in a demure and gentle fashion. 'Oh dear, have I said the wrong thing?'

Lavinia denied everything. 'My goodness, Miss Mead, you do make the *strangest* observations.'

'You must have the wrong address, Miss Mead,' added Elvira.

Miss Mead ploughed ahead. 'Oh, well I heard that Mr Walloman had found a body in the library.'

Shockwaves bounced around the room even impacting Sir Henry. 'A body! A dead body?' he asked with growing interest.

Lavinia couldn't hold back her pathetic laugh. 'Oh it's just a little joke Sir Henry; it's not true at all.'

Sir Henry caught the scent. 'I say, Archie—spot of bother—what?'

Elvira lost it. 'Please,' she pleaded, 'there is no body. It's all a terrible misunderstanding.'

Miss Mead looked confused. 'Oh, you mean there *hasn't* been a murder?'

Archie and his mother and daughter couldn't find the words. All wanted the visitors to leave—now—and the subject to be forgotten. But before they could speak, Agatha took control.

'Sir Henry, Miss Mead,' she addressed the visitors. 'I think it's time for the truth.'

The Wallomans bit their tongues and, at the same time, learnt to loathe the interloper, Agatha Crispie, with a new and searing hatred. She was about to grass on them and bring down hell fire and damnation on the fine name and household of Walloman. Ah, perhaps the bit about a fine name should be redacted.

Archie panicked. 'Agatha!'

Elvira couldn't say please. 'No!'

Lavinia demanded a response. 'Don't!'

The visitors sat poleaxed. The news of the murder was impressive in itself but more so was the over-the-top reaction of the household. Agatha resumed control.

'We would like both of you to solve a murder,' she said and stopped the clocks. The visitors reacted.

'I say,' said Sir Henry.

'Oh dear,' said Miss Mead.

As Agatha spoke, the Wallomans began to change their personality. 'As a writer of mysteries, I have invented a crime.'

Heads lifted, expressions changed, and a feeling of hope drifted down from Heaven filling and inspiring many a Walloman breast.

'Did you say invented?' asked Henry.

Agatha nodded. 'Yes, Sir Henry, you see I write murder mysteries.'

Archie embraced his wife's confession with enthusiasm. 'Yes, of course, I should have explained. Agatha has *invented* a mystery. It's only a *pretend* murder.'

Henry was super impressed whereas Miss Mead's expression and thus her mind were inscrutable.

Lavinia and Elvira took the hint from Archie. 'She's extremely good at inventing,' added Lavinia with far too much false enthusiasm.

Elvira was bursting with insincere zeal and made a terrible liar. 'She's a brilliant inventor of made-up stories.'

Agatha seized this new-found support and ran with it. She addressed the visiting official sleuth. 'And who better to solve my invented mystery than the brilliant mind of an outstanding policeman?'

Finally the penny dropped and Henry climbed aboard. 'Oh, it's a *pretend* murder—I say—what!'

Archie reckoned relief had never tasted so sweet and went a tad overboard. 'Yes, yes and Agatha's stories are so good. Aren't they family?' What a leading, leading question.

'Good?' challenged Lavinia. 'They're better than good. Why, I can't put them down.' Her statement ranked within the world's ten most outrageous lies.

Elvira so wanted to help herself and save her life in aristocratic circles. 'Would you believe her pen name is Agatha Crispie?'

Miss Mary Mead had shown no reaction to anything thus far but Agatha's pen name prompted a response involving mild shock.

'Agatha *Crispie*? Oh.'

Agatha's joy overflowed. 'I'd be delighted, Sir Henry if you would examine my plot and point out any of its weaknesses.'

Sir Henry's grin created new creases in his skull. 'Righto—jolly good—slightest flaw—will spot—what?'

'Then please join Miss Mead and observe from over there,' said Agatha indicating.

Henry nodded and stood beside the seated Miss Mead.

'Good show—capital—top hole—what?' he said moving into position, enjoying his new challenge.

Agatha ran the show. Her family seethed, their contempt for the interloper peaked at record levels, but beneath the surface they knew Agatha's stupid game was their best chance, their *only* chance of having what they believed was a real murder dismissed, and shoved firmly under the carpet.

Without any warmth, Agatha smiled at her family. 'Now I need four characters over here,' she said indicating Lavinia's chair. No-one moved. To follow any order or request from that horrid woman was never going to happen. Agatha made a face and called their bluff.

'Of course if I can't find four volunteers, we'll forget the *pretend* murder and talk about the other incident in the library.'

The response was immediate, even overwhelming. Archie moved towards his mother. As usual he overdid the false sincerity. 'I'll help, Agatha. Gosh, this should be fun.'

'Oh yes,' added Elvira with not even a scintilla of sincerity as she sat closer to her grandmother. 'What can I do to help, Stepmother?'

Lavinia sounded ridiculous. 'Am I in the right place, Agatha ... dear?'

Lavinia calling her hated daughter-in-law 'dear' took the biscuit. Any pretence of sincerity disappeared long ago, if it ever existed. But Agatha accepted their fake sincerity because she had other fish to fry. The plot of her new mystery was about to be examined by a top Scotland Yard detective, Sir Henry Dithering. No, *top* is incorrect.

But something or someone was missing. Agatha needed a fourth character to re-enact her mystery. She spied her maid in the corner.

'Pimms, we need a fourth for bridge.'

The family ground their teeth realising the hag from below stairs was not only still in the room but would now be a part of the re-enactment. As Pimms moved to the hated family members, she mimicked the guest of honour who was too thick to realise.

'Righto—jolly good—top hole—what?'

So the four characters were clustered together in their part of the library with the two detectives at the other end of the room, observing. Agatha bubbled with anticipation. 'Excellent,' she said and began to tell her tale.

'One night four friends are playing bridge.' She indicated herself. 'A fifth friend is nearby.' Agatha moved to the drinks cabinet and collected an empty tray, pretending there were four glasses thereon. She took the tray of make-believe glasses towards the acting quartet.

'As the game progresses, the fifth person moves to the card players and hands each a glass of wine.'

She mimed handing a glass to each player who all took it with varying degrees of disinterest. Pimms examined her imaginary glass, looking peeved because it was empty. Agatha moved between the detectives and the actors, preparing to announce the highlight of the mystery.

'The game continues until, without warning, the card players collapse.' No-one moved. This was because of two things; the players had no idea what Agatha was talking about, and three of them hated the author with a passion. Agatha threatened the quartet with her eyes. 'They collapse,' she repeated. Message received and understood so Pimms dropped her head, playing dead. Reluctantly, the Wallomans followed. Agatha's excitement peaked and she addressed the detectives.

'Each card player is dead. But how? Were they poisoned, and if so, with what? *How* were they killed and *who* is the murderer?' She turned to the actors. 'Thank you, everyone; you may come alive now.'

The "actors" revived and looked disgusted with Agatha and her, what they considered to be a childish prank. Agatha was bubbling. The Wallomans knew even the slowest of sleuths and the dimmest of detectives would solve this pathetic plot in an instant. *Her tales are terrible*, they thought or rather knew.

Agatha addressed the man who once solved crimes for a living when based at Scotland Yard. 'And that, Sir Henry, is my plot. I hope you found it interesting.'

Everyone looked at the former detective. It was time to officially reveal the so-called writer Agatha Crispie as the talentless fraud she is and always has been.

'Did you say interesting?' asked Sir Henry.

Chapter 12

LIKE MANY WRITERS, Agatha struggled with criticism. She poured her heart and soul into her writing only to have it ridiculed, rejected, or worse, ignored. But this was different. This involved explaining her mystery to a former police detective from Scotland Yard. If he liked and approved of it, surely publishers would likewise be impressed. Ah, but what if he found fault? What if he damned her work with faint praise? And worse, would he steady her when she collapsed at the brutality of his savage review?

Her body in the library mystery fooled her husband and maid. But this latest effort was, certainly for all her family, palpably pathetic. It fooled no-one. Even the expert, Sir Henry, must surely destroy the abysmal plot putting Agatha Crispie out of her misery once and for all. Oh, be kind, Sir Henry. Go easy on the poor, struggling artist.

Agatha held her breath as the review came in. 'Did I find it interesting?' he asked. 'Interesting?' She grimaced and stopped breathing. The family prepared to gloat. Some were ready to cheer Sir Henry. 'Dear lady,' he announced, 'it's breathtakingly brilliant.'

Agatha couldn't move. The others suffered from dropped-jaw syndrome. Even Miss Mead found her eyes growing larger.

'Oh, Sir Henry,' gushed Agatha. 'Do you really think so?'

Henry was away. 'Madam, I've studied hundreds of murder cases but *never* have I seen so complex and baffling a scenario as this. You have a gift, madam, a rare and natural talent for story-telling.' He stepped back and saluted. 'I salute the soon-to-be famous crime writer, Agatha Crispie!'

Agatha was speechless; so too the others but for different reasons. Archie recovered first. He should have said nothing and bundled Henry out the door but Archie couldn't stand by and let his wife win rich and, what he considered to be, totally undeserved plaudits.

'Come on, Henry, old chap; it *was* a tad obvious.'

Lavinia scoffed. 'Of course it was obvious. We all saw Agatha serve the poisoned drinks meaning she alone *has* to be the murderer.'

'Genius,' said Henry. His response meant incredulity ran amok. 'First rule in detection; beware the obvious.'

'But everyone died at exactly the same time,' argued Elvira. 'What could be more unbelievable than that?'

Sir Henry answered the questions with confidence even glee. 'And those simultaneous deaths are another peerless piece of plotting designed to fool even the sharpest detective. The murderer used different poisons.'

Agatha was a bystander while her family tore into the plot. Now she found new confidence, and supported her champion, Sir Henry.

'Yes!' she cried excitedly, 'that's exactly what *did* happen!'

She and Sir Henry were on the same ridiculous wavelength.

Henry rammed home his theory. 'And, don't you know, poisons react in different ways and at different times, what!'

Agatha was a tiny step away from dancing. 'They do, they do!'

Pleased as punch Henry delivered the denouement.

'And the murderer, who studied the drinking habits of the victims over the last sixteen years, secretly calculated their respective body temperatures in a well-furnished sitting room in the south-west of England on a sunny Friday in mid-July, and so knew *precisely* how much of which poison to deliver simultaneously to produce the same lethal effect.'

Agatha combined delight with amazement. If she were honest, she hadn't gone as far in her thinking as the pompous Sir Henry explained; nowhere near it if truth be told. But what he deduced, guessed or, more likely made up, gave her spirits a huge boost. She could be a writer of mysteries after all. She shook her head as emotion flooded her body before thanking her new mentor.

'Sir Henry, what can I say?'

Elvira spoke softly but loud enough for her family to hear. 'Say he's a fruitcake.'

Henry pointed at Agatha. 'You madam, have worked in a pharmacy. You know your drugs, what!'

'I have and do and you, sir, have cracked the case.' He was as chuffed as Agatha. What a team. She should engage him as her literary agent; or then again, perhaps not.

Elvira couldn't stand all this praise being heaped on her stepmother a moment longer. She gave Henry's review a stinging fail. 'Cracked the case? You cannot be serious. The plot is ludicrous.'

This comment was heard by all with everyone sensing hostility. The gloves were off, and Archie needed to kill any potential problem. So far the dead body in the library had avoided inspection, and now was the time to shut down the whole shebang. Archie went to Henry and placed an arm around the dithering Dithering.

'Oh, well done, Henry, old bean. You deserve a real drink. In my study, old chap. Come along—tally-ho—what!'

Henry was easily persuaded and the chaps set off.

'Oh, rather—jolly good show,' chirped the former police officer.

The duo had hardly moved when Agatha let out an almighty cry.

'No!' The men froze and faced the distraught writer. Everyone stared at her. 'No! I've failed.'

It was natural for the others to speak as one. 'Failed?' they asked, and wanted to add, "Tell us something we don't know".

Agatha explained. 'If Sir Henry can unravel it so easily, so might my readers.'

Lavinia spoke bluntly. 'What readers? Tell me their names.'

Elvira belittled her stepmother. 'You need a publisher first.'

Henry moved to comfort the writer of whom he predicted a bright future. 'Come, come, dear lady. Your average reader doesn't have the genius of an experienced police officer. Why the amateur sleuth Miss Mary Mead here could never have solved your mystery. Miss Mead?'

Everyone looked at the, until now, silent Miss Mead. She spoke in a calm and measured voice. 'I could certainly have never used your logic, Sir Henry,' she said with barely a scintilla of irony.

Henry continued comforting Agatha. 'Rest assured, madam, your plot is foolproof.'

'Are you sure?' asked Agatha desperate for encouragement.

'Madam, I'm positive,' replied Henry.

'But I read once that only fools are positive.'

Henry was taken aback and queried the matter. 'Oh, are you sure?'

'I'm positive,' said Agatha with a straight face, and her family witnessed Agatha's literary suicide note.

The deadlock was broken when the other visitor joined the discussion. 'Perhaps you might make one small alteration,' she said.

Archie wanted this discussion shut down. 'Oh come now, Miss Mead; surely you should stick to pruning cardigans and knitting roses.' He was as bad as Dithering.

Miss Mead explained. 'One tiny change would make your mystery genuinely mysterious.' She paused. 'You could reverse the roles.'

The others came alive. Henry's explanation of Agatha's unbelievable plot was more incredible than the plot itself but Miss Mead's comments brought the mystery to life.

Agatha wanted more. 'You mean, make the fifth person a man?'

Henry attacked. 'No, no, no—men are hopeless with poison.'

Elvira spoke under her breath. 'You don't need, "with poison".'

Miss Mead explained her suggestion. 'Actually I thought the fifth person could be the victim.'

Everyone responded at once with volume. 'What?'

'The victim?' said a confused Agatha. 'The murderer is murdered?'

Henry stepped in to fix the confusion. 'Oh dear, the misguided novice,' he said and addressed Miss Mead. 'Madam, the more victims you have, the more complex the plot.'

Mary knew better, much better. 'And equally, sir, the more suspects you have, the more tricky the solution.' She stumped Henry. 'And if the fifth person is the one to die, you'd have a *real* whodunit.

Henry was thrown. 'A real what did you say? A whodunit?'

No-one spoke as the spinster in tweed, unremarkable hat and sensible shoes tied them all in knots. The broken silence came from an unexpected source.

'Oh I understand,' said Pimms who became the focus of attention. The others stared at her. *Why is she in the room? How did she get in?* Pimms gave a weak smile and waited for the full barrage attack.

'Fetch my tea and a drink for Sir Henry,' snapped Lavinia.

Pimms had no choice. Grumbling or mumbling or possibly both, she made her exit. 'Spoil sport,' was heard.

Elvira threw in her poshness. 'We do apologise, Sir Henry. That woeful woman is leaving our service.'

'Today,' snapped Lavinia.

Agatha was lost in the responses to her tale. She spoke aloud trying to sort matters in her mind. 'So the fifth person is murdered and the murderer could be any one of the four card players?'

Miss Mead explained. 'Indeed, or to make it *really* complicated, you could have more than one murderer.'

This was the last straw for Henry. Meddling amateurs didn't ever understand. 'Oh dearie, me,' he said struggling to contain a grin. 'You've all missed the perfectly obvious clue.' He paused, watching while everyone hung on his next sentence. 'Another person's in the room.'

The others were stunned. '*Another* person?' asked Archie.

'*What* other person?' asked Elvira.

'And where in the room?' asked a confused Lavinia.

Henry couldn't understand why his explanation wasn't accepted. 'Why, any person, anywhere. They could be crouched under the desk or behind the settee or covered by a curtain.' He pointed, others looked and saw nothing. They gave up.

Not so, Agatha. She understood. 'Of course, yes! A person armed with a blowpipe and poisoned darts.'

'Exactly,' said Henry giving Agatha support.

'And wearing a pink tutu,' added a sarcastic Elvira.

'While shaving a turnip,' added Lavinia with copious sarcasm.

Henry celebrated believing his "expert" theories were supported by his fans. He didn't do irony or sarcasm. He didn't do much at all. 'Yes, well done!' he cried, then felt inspired and pointed. 'Or maybe a minor earth tremor took place in that precise part of the room.'

The others looked where Henry pointed. The floor coverings and furniture slumbered in a deep sleep.

Lavinia became incredulous. 'They were killed by an earthquake?'

Agatha sparkled. The brainstorming session produced a plethora of new ideas. 'Yes! Simultaneously!'

'And at the same time,' said Henry who became serious. 'Ladies and gentlemen, beware of mystery writers depicting the police as dim-witted plodders who wouldn't know their truncheon from a teapot. I mean, look at me. Would anyone ever call me thick?'

A serious pause and riotous silence settled in the library. The humans looked at the grinning former Scotland Yard detective. Miss Mead spoke for the gathering.

'I was never much good at rhetorical questions,' she said.

Henry's grin continued. He'd done it again, so Archie stepped in to prevent Henry's stupidity flooding the library carpets.

'I say, excellent work, old chap. What a stroke of luck, you being in the area.'

Lavinia wanted all visitors gone. 'You have to admit, Miss Mead, a policeman's mind is a wonder to behold.'

'I could not have put it better,' she said without irony or sarcasm.

Agatha continued to bask in her success. 'I'm ever so grateful, Sir Henry and Miss Mead. You've both helped me re-write my mystery.'

Henry wagged a finger and grinned. 'And I trust I'll receive the appropriate acknowledgment once the jolly thing's published, what?'

Henry chuckled and Archie joined him but slipped back into mocking his wife. 'Oh, of course; the *moment* it's published.'

Both men laughed but for different reasons. Henry thought he was bright, and Archie thought he was brighter. Agatha wanted advice.

'Sir Henry, please allow me to outline another of my murder plots.'

The Wallomans fired their response as one. 'No!'

Henry loved being the centre of attention and was deaf to the family's protest. 'Dear lady, I'd be delighted—what!'

The routine was halted when Pimms knocked on the library door.

'It'll be Pimms,' said Archie wanting the maid's entrance to kill any possible fight developing in front of the visitors. He called. 'Pimms!' No-one appeared. Archie apologised. 'I'm afraid she's awfully slow.'

'She's leaving,' said Lavinia as the door opened.

'Ah, at last,' said Archie as Pimms arrived with the drinks trolley. She appeared to have had an accident, as her left hand was wrapped in a white bandage. She stopped pushing and addressed Archie.

'Sorry, sir; I had to find the best whisky for Sir Henry. The first three bottles was not up to scratch.' She prepared to pour a glass for Sir Henry when Agatha noticed her bandaged hand.

'Pimms! What's happened to your hand?'

She looked at it. 'Oh it's that darn mousetrap, Madam. It keeps on keeping on.'

Archie usually took no notice of domestic matters but this saga had been running for ages.

'Haven't you caught that blasted mouse, yet?' he asked.

His mother and daughter rolled their eyes with so mundane a matter being discussed anywhere other than in the kitchen, and by anyone other than servants.

Pimms explained. 'I'm afraid our mousetrap has a life of its own.'

'You have to put it in the right place,' said Archie and Lavinia's teeth could be heard to grind.

'We have the best results when it's set in the West End,' replied Pimms struggling with her bandaged hand.

'We have a mousetrap, Sir Henry, which has performed for this family for generations,' said Agatha.

'Well they say a good mousetrap will last forever,' said the former Scotland Yard man.

'Now then Henry,' said Archie, 'the usual for you?'

'Rather,' said Henry.

'Right, Pimms,' said Archie, 'tea for the ladies, a scotch and soda for Sir Henry, and I'll have a body in the library.'

Chapter 13

SILENCE BOUNCED AROUND THE ROOM. Helped by having a bandaged hand, Pimms dropped whatever she was holding—crash; and the gasp from everyone, including poor old Archie, meant that what was never meant to happen, happened. Archie could have kicked himself. He continued to worry so much about the former stiff on the sofa he lost control of his brain and thus his speech.

Miss Mead was the first to respond. 'Oh, do forgive me, Mr Walloman, but I was sure I heard you order a body in the library.'

Everyone stared at the patriarch. He struggled, his mind raced and he said the first thing he could think of. 'Ah, yes, it's a new cocktail.' He pointed a shaking finger at Pimms. 'I'll have my usual, Pimms.'

She had no idea what he meant and no desire to help him. It was a mess of his own making. 'I'm afraid I've forgotten your usual, sir?'

Archie feigned annoyance. 'Oh you know, my usual cocktail; a body in the library.'

She milked his misery. 'And will that be shaken or stabbed, sir?'

Archie appeared to be cracking. His mother and daughter could not believe that the horrendous truth they had avoided for so long would now be revealed right at the death. They tried desperately to rescue the situation with Lavinia leading the charge.

'And how are your meads, Miss Rose?' Lavinia bit her tongue.

This nonsensical question, rather than distract from Archie's faux pas, only highlighted the matter. Elvira attempted a rescue.

'Pimms, I'd like coffee in my tea.' Elvira bit her tongue.

The tension kept building. Both visitors, even Sir Henry, sensed something was amiss.

'Body in the library—meads, Miss Rose—coffee in my tea? I say, Archie, what's going on old boy—what?'

Agatha felt fantastic. Another person, not her, her husband no less, had raised her other mystery, the stiff on the settee. Now she could have both her plots tested by a former Scotland Yard detective.

'Oh, Sir Henry, it's another of my mysteries. Please will you investigate this one as well?'

Even *he* was struggling to keep up. '*More* make-believe?'

Then it happened. The pretence collapsed. Archie, who could not deny the truth a moment longer, wanted to confess, *had* to confess.

'No, no, no,' he blubbed. 'It's all true.' He looked pathetic.

His mother fumed. She demanded he pull himself together, refuse to say another word, and act like a man, all with one word. 'Archibald!' she growled. She failed.

'It's a scandal, Henry,' said Archie. 'If this gets out, I'm finished!'

His mother and daughter as good as died. Their good name—well hardly good, and only in their eyes—was in danger of being defiled, with nothing they could do to prevent the impending disaster.

Naturally Henry showed concern. 'Spot of bother, old chap, what?'

Despite his distress, Archie managed to speak. 'Yes, yes, yes.' He paused and the others froze, staring at the middle-aged child. 'We *did* have a murder!'

Henry struggled to understand. 'A *real* murder? I say.'

Miss Mead understood and was way ahead of the game. 'Oh dear.'

Archie regained a sense of reality and explained. 'But the body's vanished, Henry; it up and disappeared. It was right there on the settee, I left the room for a few seconds, and when I came back, it had gone missing. We asked Miss Mead to help before you arrived.'

Henry took over. Nothing was too difficult for this outstanding detective. 'Jolly good—solve case—be discreet—what!' He addressed Miss Mead. 'Kindly observe, dear lady; the master at work.'

'I'm much obliged, Sir Henry,' she said wondering, as were the others, about how big a dog's breakfast he would make of this case.

'Right-y-o, so who discovered the body?' asked Henry.

Archie sheepishly raised a hand. 'I did.'

'Splendid. Where was it—what?'

Archie was both humiliated and distressed. His reputation as a wonderfully successful businessman and golfer who didn't cheat—often—was about to be shattered. He spoke in barely a whisper.

'It was on the settee. It was very dark.'

Henry moved into his work. 'What, midnight, two a.m.?'

'No, broad daylight; the murdered woman asked me to close the curtains.'

Well if the situation wasn't monumentally horrendous already, it certainly became so now. Lavinia and Elvira discovered apoplexy causing even their clothes to become uncomfortable.

'Archibald! How could you?' gasped his mother.

Archie's explanation made matters worse. Could they become worse? 'She was a reporter, a Miss Dorothy S. Layers.'

Elvira wanted to die. Miss Mead expressed mild shock. 'Oh, my goodness,' she said in her unflappable tone.

Archie tried and failed to justify his behaviour. 'She was recommended by Lord Peter Fancy.'

Lavinia gave it to him. 'I don't care if she was recommended by Buckingham Palace, your behaviour is unforgiveable.'

Elvira had a serious question. 'Is murder a crime if the victim is a reporter?'

The true nature of the Wallomans stood up and shouted. "Look at me! We're the important ones!" they screamed. Henry ignored their comments. He wanted to re-enact the scene. He clapped his hands. 'Right-y-o, let's have the room exactly as it was?' Nobody moved. Nobody wanted to move. 'Come now, chop, chop and all that.'

Pimms went to the curtains and closed them. Agatha moved to the light switch. The room became dark.

'This is absurd,' snapped Lavinia.

Archie remembered. 'Ah, the light was turned on.'

Agatha flicked the switch and the darkened room was lit.

'Jolly good,' said Henry. 'And where was the body, what?'

Archie pointed. 'It was right there, stretched out on the settee.'

'Good show,' said Henry looking at the Walloman women. 'Ladies, we need a volunteer.' Elvira moved at lightning speed to avoid being involved. Lavinia dared anyone to even think of her.

Archie chose a volunteer. 'Agatha, you can be the dead body.'

Indignation reared its head. 'Me?' protested Agatha. 'You said she was a plain, plump frump!'

'Yes, but you're the right height.'

Flashing daggers with her eyes, Agatha sat on the settee. Henry was pleased with his investigation. 'Excellent,' he said. 'Now, what happened next?'

Archie sat on the settee beside his wife. 'I was sitting on the settee when the reporter admired a painting.' Archie looked at Agatha. 'That's you,' he said advising her of the role.

'Which painting?' she asked, now enjoying her plot being tested.

'By the door,' he said and Agatha moved there awaiting instructions. 'The reporter was admiring the painting when suddenly the lights went out.'

'Good show,' said Henry heading to the light switch. He flicked it and the room went dark. Lavinia and Elvira gasped. 'What next?'

Archie stood and moved to the light switch. 'I went to the light switch.' He collides slightly with Henry on his travels. They muttered apologies. 'When here,' said Archie, 'I switched on the light.'

'Jolly good,' said Henry as the light returned.

Gasps sounded in stereo. Everyone stared at the settee upon which Agatha reclined in exactly the same position she was found before. The knife, scarf, peg and wheat were missing but to Archie, it was deja vu.

'Oh my God!' he cried and hurried to the back of the settee. 'Agatha!' Lavinia and Elvira were disgusted and even a tad afraid. This had all the characteristics of being real.

Henry felt excited. 'So you discovered the body. Was she dead?'

'Of course she was dead,' blurted Archie. 'She'd been stabbed, strangled and suffocated.'

'In that order?' asked the incredibly stupid ex-detective.

'How would I know?' squawked a deeply disturbed Archie.

'Excellent,' said Henry. 'So what did you do with the body?'

Archie struggled to remember what he did as the agony of what happened, flooded back and upset him. 'Nothing! I called for help and ...' He turned and looked at Pimms. 'And then Pimms arrived.'

Pimms looked defiant. 'What?'

'You came in and saw the body.'

'No comment,' said Pimms thinking she was in a police station.

Archie snapped. 'You were there!' He pointed. 'Right there.'

Pimms felt trapped. 'Oh yes, I came in and saw Mrs Walloman, er, *Mr* Walloman ... and the body.'

Henry probed. 'And you're sure the woman was dead?'

Pimms became nervous. She had the ability to make life super embarrassing for her mistress. 'Yes, at the time I did.'

'At the time?' bellowed Archie. 'What are you talking about? Oh, of course, I forgot. Ten minutes later she magically came alive again.'

Pimms snarled. 'I never said that.' She spoke to Sir Henry. 'He's putting words in me mouth, m'lud.' Henry beamed from the bench.

Archie stood his ground. 'Of course she was dead. She even had a clothes-peg on her nose and a pocket full of rye.'

'I see,' said super sleuth Dithering. 'This might be a domestic homicide involving washing and whisky.' The onlookers were speechless. 'Then what happened?'

Pimms remembered. 'Mr Walloman went to tell the others and that's when ...' Pimms stalled. Agatha, flat on her back, stared at her.

Henry wanted to know. 'Yes? And that's when what?'

The others were frantic to know; everyone except Agatha.

'What happened?' demanded Lavinia.

'Speak,' snapped Elvira.

Pimms decided to tell the truth. 'That's when ...'

Chapter 14

BEFORE PIMMS COULD ANSWER, Agatha sat up and spoke. 'May I sit up, please? It's not much fun being dead.'

Henry moved as if in a trance. He knew he'd had a vision, and darted about pointing at people, warning them. 'Don't speak. Nobody speak. Absolute silence. I'm certain I've solved it—what!'

Surprise was universal. 'You have?' asked every other human, desperate for news. Even the birds in the garden fell silent.

Henry oozed confidence, his experience enabling him to unravel the trickiest of cases. 'I believe a second person entered this room, probably a tall, dark stranger, someone who has nothing to do with this outstanding, impeccably-behaved family, and who muttered a few words about unrequited love, and then carried the body off through ...' He wasn't sure where until he spied the destination. He pointed and as he spoke, the others pointed and spoke with him.

'Those French windows!'

Henry took their joining in as proof of his extraordinary claim. Archie reinforced Henry's statement when he, Archie, realised the description was correct in every detail.

'But that's exactly what *did* happen.'

Henry grinned. Of course. Pimms couldn't believe what she heard.

'Blimey, the nincompoop's a novelist,' she muttered.

Henry basked in his own self-importance. 'Of course this sort of deduction is elementary for an experienced, first-class detective.'

Lavinia and Elvira were over the moon. 'Brilliant detective work, Sir Henry; the work of a genius,' said the matriarch.

'Absolutely super,' glowed Elvira.

Henry mopped up the loose ends. 'The local police will make routine enquires but I see no reason why this highly respectable household should ever be troubled again.'

Archie and his mother were mightily relieved. Elvira gushed.

'Oh thank you, Sir Henry, thank you; you have saved my honour and my spotless reputation.' Sadly for Elvira, self-praise is no praise.

Henry was delighted to have assisted Archie's child bride.

Agatha, however, saw her murder plot being pushed aside. She protested. 'But if there's been a murder, what happened to the body? We can't just forget it.'

'We can and we have already forgotten it,' snarled Lavinia. She glared at her daughter-in-law. 'Even *you* have forgotten it!'

Archie took the mater's side. 'Agatha, we've just witnessed the work of a truly magnificent detective. It's now time to move on.'

'But Sir Henry, are you *sure* you're correct?' asked Agatha.

Henry was beyond certain. 'Madam, in fiction the police may be flawed, described as dim and dithering but in real life, we sparkle.'

'Hear, hear,' said Lavinia and Elvira as one.

Now all this re-enactment and summation by Henry left the other visitor out in the cold. Miss Mary Mead sat there, silent throughout, being ignored. She was the one invited to solve the mystery, and Sir Henry had stolen her thunder. Lavinia spotted this and felt sorry for the village's spinster sleuth. Lavinia felt sorry for someone? Really?

'Well Miss Mead, it appears the police are intelligent and street smart after all. Sir Henry has put you out of a job.'

Miss Mead agreed—or did she? 'So it would seem. But I can't help wondering how the lights went out.'

Her remark tickled Henry's funny bone. 'Oh dear; we have a question from the enthusiastic amateur. Why it could have been an electrical storm, a faulty wire; even spontaneous combustion.'

What!? Henry would have been better saying nowt. It was the story of his life as the poor chap kept digging.

Miss Mead persisted. 'But is it possible the lights were turned off by the murdered woman?'

Shock exploded. Several audible gasps sounded. How could that possibly occur? And the question had to be asked; was Miss Mead's fine reputation obtained by fraudulent means? Is she a phoney?

Henry couldn't hide his grin. 'Well, there you have it, what?—the part-time, well-meaning and hopelessly misguided do-gooder.'

Archie should have left well alone but he too couldn't help himself. 'What I don't understand is *why* she was murdered?'

'Archibald,' growled his mother.

Henry dug himself a deeper hole. 'And as she was murdered, how could she find her way to the lights in the dark?' His idiocy and lack of logic plumbed new depths.

Miss Mead had a theory. 'Could the woman be already familiar with the layout of the room?'

'Already?' queried Sir Henry. 'What, before or after she died?'

Lavinia sensed the amateur was onto something and worried. She scoffed trying to kill Miss Mead's suggestion. 'Oh, Miss Mead, these wild guesses have gone far enough.'

'Yes,' added Elvira. 'Sir Henry has solved the mystery. The investigation is over—it's finished.'

'Finished?' asked Miss Mead. 'How could it be finished if it didn't even start? This may well be a case of no body, no murder.'

Again the little old lady from the village came up with a seriously challenging comment. Henry was way out of his depth.

'Oh I say; what a quaint dear lady you are.'

Mary nailed it. 'And the only person who can answer that question is Pimms.'

Wow! Miss Mead delivered a powerful true statement and a possible solution to the mystery. Everyone turned from Miss Mead to Pimms who felt all those eyes burning into her body. Agatha's eyes were more a plea than a threat, and Archie seized the moment.

'Yes! That's true! Pimms was alone, here in this room, when the body disappeared. She's the one person who knows what happened.'

Lavinia didn't care and wanted the case shut down yesterday. 'We can't rely on a senile servant.'

Elvira cared even less. 'She probably invented the entire ridiculous tale herself. The maid has caught the fiction disease!'

Archie persisted. He knew what he saw on the settee in this room. 'Well come on, Pimms, let's be having you—the truth—speak!'

And so the moment arrived. Agatha's daring plan to test a plot device was about to be exposed. She planned and executed the whole thing and the only person who knew the truth and nothing but the truth was the elderly, sarcastic but loyal domestic. The pressure was intense. Pimms decided to tell all and tension provided a drum roll.

Agatha got in first and spoke loudly adding a waving finger to make her point. 'And remember Pimms, we are currently considering your employment.'

Poor Pimms; the only friend she had in this household—the world—was now threatening her. Or was it a plea?

'Well,' Pimms began; looking at the various faces, 'I came into the room and ...' She hesitated.

Archie demanded the truth. 'And?'

'And ...' She cringed in fear and pain, clasping her bandaged hand to signify the cause of her latest behaviour. 'Oh the pain,' she moaned. 'It keeps on and on. It's ...' She collapsed on the settee and gasped, '... the mousetrap!'

The room exclaimed as one. 'The mousetrap!?'

Agatha swooped to her maid's side offering help and comfort. Henry and even Archie did the gentlemanly thing, moving closer.

'I think she's fainted,' said Archie not wanting to stand too close.

'It may be fatal,' said Lavinia resorting to prayer—for the demise of Pimms.

'Oh how sad,' said Elvira, 'she's actually dead.'

Henry liked playing *Doctors and Nurses*. 'No, I can feel a pulse,' he said looking in her left ear from a foot away. He failed basic anatomy. He failed everything.

Archie didn't care for Pimms but dying on the job and in his home would be tricky to explain. If he were alone, he would've taken the body out to the nearby woods and left it for ramblers to discover. It was a tragic accident—natural causes of course. 'Come on, Pimms,' he said urging her to remain alive for at least another two minutes.

Agatha went to her desk. 'I have a list of doctors.'

She stopped when Pimms groaned. Archie called. 'Wait! She's coming round.'

Doctor Dithering took control. 'Stand back, give her air.'

As Pimms was examined, Miss Mead stood and announced. 'Oh good heavens; is that the time? I really must be going.'

Attention switched from Pimms to Miss Mead. 'So soon, Miss Mead?' asked Lavinia. 'Are you sure you won't stay for tea?' she said not wanting the female detective to remain a second more.

'Thank you, no. I'm expecting Missus McCulligiddy on the 5.40 from Stuffington.'

Henry took the hint. His work was done here and justice needed his brilliance elsewhere. 'And I too must be cutting along—what!' He smiled at the Walloman women. 'So nice to have met you, ladies. And pray don't concern yourselves over that dead body.' He tapped his nose and grinned. 'Dumb's the word, what?'

Archie headed for the library door. 'I'll see you out.' He escorted Miss Mead and Henry, opening the door for his visitors.

Lavinia called. 'Goodbye, Miss Mead. Do call again.'

Elvira glared at her grandmother.

'Thank you,' said Miss Mead. 'You're most kind. Goodbye.'

She waved and left and Henry turned back at the door. He waved to the residents. 'Cheerio—tally ho—what!'

Archie followed the visitors out and closed the door. Agatha remained beside Pimms on the settee. Lavinia sprang from her favourite chair and stood beside the settee clutching her stick as a weapon. Elvira moved to the other end of the settee as grandmother and granddaughter prepared to vilify Agatha and her revolting maid. This was not going to be pretty.

Chapter 15

LAVINIA LED THE CHARGE. A person of her breeding would never swear or spit; at least not in public. But right now, after all the brouhaha over Agatha's trashy tales and ridiculous re-enactments, Lavinia's breeding vanished and her daughter-in-law copped it.

Lavinia gave a polite version of her rudeness. 'You stupid, moronic woman; you and your childish games are a stain on humankind.'

Elvira trained at the same school of spite. 'Your imbecilic behaviour is dangerous. You're worse than your dreadful, drunken dogsbody of a maid.' Then Grannie took the reins again.

'Have you no shame? Do you actually enjoy being humiliated?'

'You haven't heard the last of this. Both of you!' added Elvira.

The door flew open and Archie entered enraged. As he strode to the settee, his family kept attacking with Lavinia still leading.

'And if your ridiculous charade ever becomes public, you'll regret it as long as you live.'

'Which won't be very long,' sneered Elvira.

Archie was now in place and took his turn. 'You stupid, moronic woman; you and your childish games are a stain on humankind.'

Lavinia's rage increased thanks to her son's repetition. 'I've already said that.'

Archie fired. 'You're worse than your dreadful, drunken dogsbody of a maid.'

Elvira now hated her father as well. 'I've already said that.'

Archie let it all out. 'Your pathetic mysteries are an abysmal failure. *You're* an abysmal failure!'

Finally Agatha fought back. Her replies oozed emotion. 'Yes but it was *you* who found the body in the library.'

Lavinia roared. 'There *was* no body in the library.'

'My mystery fooled you *and* the police,' said Agatha. 'You're all angry because I tricked the lot of you.'

Incensed, Archie fired back. 'I wasn't fooled for an instant. I know exactly what happened.'

Agatha scoffed. 'Oh Archie, you should be writing fiction.'

The slanging match ended abruptly when a person knocked on the library door. Everyone froze and looked at one another. Who on Earth could this be? *Not another burst from Sir Henry, please!*

Pimms took advantage of the break in play, stood and headed to the door. 'I know, I'll go, I'm the maid.'

She didn't move far as Archie bounded after her and blocked her path. 'Ah no! I haven't finished with you.' His threatening glare put the wind up Pimms who remained stuck to the spot. Archie turned, strode to the door and opened it still enraged. His personality underwent a radical change as he spoke with a mild voice. 'Miss Mead,' he said and stepped back to allow her entry.

'Oh, I'm so sorry,' she said. 'I seem to have misplaced my spectacles.'

The family was relieved but wary. Lavinia carried on acting the concerned and polite hostess. 'Oh well, we'll all look, shall we?'

Archie, Lavinia and Elvira pretended to search when all they wanted was the silly old biddy to be gone so their unbridled assault on Agatha and that creature, the maid, could resume.

Miss Mead appeared to search as well. It was a library full of pretend searchers. 'I'm always losing them. Once I even found them on top of my head.' She looked in her basket 'Good heavens; here they are in my basket.' She showed them to the others.

'Oh well done, Miss Mead,' said Archie moving to escort her, yet again, from the library.

'Thank you so much,' she said. 'One must make allowances for we forgetful old ladies.'

Agatha thanked the visitor for interrupting her trial and summary execution. 'Ah but your brain is as sharp as ever, Miss Mead.'

She was pleased. 'Do you think so? How kind. And yes, I did see the clothes-peg you left behind, Mrs Walloman. You must have dropped it in your haste to leave the room.' A deathly hush settled and time appeared to stand still. Miss Mead smiled. 'It was so nice meeting you all again. Goodbye.'

She departed with Archie close behind. 'Goodbye, Miss Mead,' he called and watched as she made her way out through the kitchen. He turned, closed the door causing its frame to wince.

Archie exploded. 'Dorothy S. Layers!' he growled pointing at Agatha and seethed, more so because he'd made such a fool of himself. '*You're* the reporter.'

Lavinia and Elvira were stunned. Pimms hid a smile.

'What?' exclaimed both grandmother and granddaughter.'

Agatha dropped her anger. 'It was only a game, Archie. Don't make such a fuss.'

'It's childish, beneath contempt and dangerous,' he bellowed.

'Dangerous?' challenged Agatha; 'but surely only to your ego.'

Lavinia loathed Agatha. 'If you were a man, I'd have you flogged.'

'All I did was experiment with the plot of a new murder mystery,' said Agatha still worried the others would do something silly.

Elvira had never hated her stepmother as she did right now. 'You have degraded us all!'

Pimms piped up. '*I* wasn't degraded.'

Archie exploded into yet another rage. He pointed at Pimms. 'You! You get out! I'll deal with you later.' Pimms looked at Archie. 'Out!'

She and Agatha exchanged a glance before Pimms began her journey to the gallows otherwise known as the kitchen.

As she departed, Lavinia gave an order. 'Oh for heaven's sake, Archibald, dismiss her now!'

'Ah no,' said Archie with a plan in mind. 'Dismissal's too good for our Pimms. I've got a special treat in mind for her.'

'May I remind you, Archie, Pimms is *my* maid and *I* control her employment,' said Agatha.

Archie became a man—well, his interpretation of a man. 'I'll thank you to be quiet, Agatha, all of you. I have something important to say.'

'And about time,' said his mother. 'Still, it's better late than never.'

Archie turned on his wife. 'Agatha, your idiotic mysteries have come close to costing this family its honour and reputation.'

'Now that is laughable,' said Agatha. 'Talk about an overreaction.'

'It's unforgivable,' sneered Elvira, '*you're* unforgivable.'

'Oh come now,' said Agatha. 'The hopeless detective thought he solved a murder which never took place, I've improved my plot, and Miss Mary Mead knows it was all a silly prank.'

'What a perfect description of your writing,' said Lavinia.

Agatha worked up a head of steam. She was sick of the cruel barbs and sarcastic comments from the family into which she married. 'Well instead of ridiculing me, why not offer some encouragement?'

As one, her three tormentors spoke, no, shouted. 'Why?'

Archie led the charge. 'You have no talent and no publisher. You are a colossal failure, and an embarrassment. Well no more. It's over, Agatha. Your writing now is dead!'

Lavinia was finally pleased to see the farce ended. 'And when do we see quality servants, Archibald?'

'And what about my social life, Father?' asked Elvira.

Archie ignored his mother and daughter and kept on at his wife. 'You rarely attend dinner engagements. You're off researching a ghastly whodunit where anyone can pick the murderer in the first chapter; no, the first page.'

'How would you know?' demanded Agatha. 'You've never read my books.'

'What books?' scoffed Elvira. 'They're piles of jumbled jottings.'

Archie continued. 'In six months you've hosted one dinner party to which only two people came.'

'You invited them,' she fired back.

'Good lord, woman, you're my wife. You're supposed to do those things.'

'A real wife *does* do those things,' added Lavinia.

Agatha fought back. 'Archibald, I am confused. A short time ago, here in this very room, you said a woman should have a career. Do you deny making such a statement?'

Archie blustered—and lied. 'Fortunately I knew all along it was you pretending to be that hysterical journalist.'

Agatha threw back her head and laughed. 'Oh Archie, please; even my worst plots have more credibility than that.'

Lavinia was bored. 'Enough! I refuse to stay in this woman's presence a moment longer.' She set off for the door speaking without looking behind her. 'Archibald, your wife's behaviour is deplorable.'

Archie copped it from every angle. 'Thank you, Mother. I can handle this.' Now not everyone would agree with that statement.

'Put your wife in her place, employ respectable servants and introduce your daughter to society; three simple tasks,' said Lavinia.

'Mother!' said Archie in despair. She tapped her stick forcing her son to traipse after her and open the door. As she departed, she glared at her son. 'Or else,' she threatened.

Archie turned to face his wife and daughter. Before he could begin his diatribe, Elvira interrupted. 'Father, I simply must say this.'

'Not now, Elvira.

'You have to consider divorce.'

Agatha fumed. 'Divorce!'

Archie defended his actions. 'But I've stopped Agatha's writing.'

'Not from her. From *me!*' said Elvira in a shrill voice.

Agatha was thrown. 'What!?'

'Don't be absurd,' said Archie with a dismissive wave of his hand.

Elvira stated her case. 'I've studied deportment and grooming. I can, with intelligence, discuss topics from tapestry to trekking in Tibet. I've read every engagement notice in *The Times* and *The Telegraph* since Armistice Day and now, because you're too weak to put your half-witted wife in her place, *my* place in society, *my whole life* is fast becoming a disaster!'

'You're behaving like a spoilt child, Elvira. You're becoming unbearable,' argued Archie.

She disagreed. 'Is Sir Edward Palliser handling your legal affairs?'

Archie lost it. 'Elvira! I forbid you to discuss these matters.'

'Why should I allow your wife's unpublished and unpublishable scribble destroy my life?'

She stomped to the door. Archie yelled. 'Enough! Elvira, *stop!*'

She did stop but before her father could say another word, she did. 'I want a divorce!'

She left in a huff with a capital H, such that the library door needed a massage. Archie thought he'd overcome a few issues but instead found himself in a right royal mess. He forgot his wife who remained, seated on the settee. He wandered about thinking aloud.

'This is worse than I thought.'

Agatha took a conciliatory approach but Archie was so worried he didn't listen.

'Archibald, I'm truly sorry for your distress, and I apologise for deceiving you as Dorothy S. Layers.'

He continued in dreamland. 'This could damage my business.'

'Your mother and daughter are clearly upset, Archie.'

He woke up, snapped out of his misery, and went on the attack. 'Right, first we deal with Pimms.'

Agatha refused. She had few no-go areas but her maid was one. 'No; she's *my* maid and I *won't* dismiss her.'

He felt for a document in one of his pockets. 'You won't and I won't. She's being transferred.'

'Transferred? What do you mean, transferred?'

He handed her a document. 'I've signed the authority. You will complete the details—immediately.'

Agatha studied the document and recoiled in shock. '*Stonydoors!* That's a hospital for the insane.'

'The owner is a friend of mine.'

'You haven't got any friends.'

Archie's temper grew white hot. 'She's off! And you will make it as soon as is humanly possible!'

'But Pimms has never worked in an asylum.'

Veins in Archie's temple throbbed. 'She's not going there to work. She'll be a patient!'

'But Pimms isn't mad!'

'Of course she is. She works for you!'

Agatha defied her husband. 'I won't do this.'

'Oh yes you will, and today. I want the document posted this afternoon.'

The couple paused. This confrontation had been building for a while; some would say since the day they wed. Archie wanted a wife for decoration and domesticity. He did not want a literary failure, or someone who played farcical pranks to support her fervent interest in writing shambolic murder mysteries.

He spoke in a softer voice but his intent was still forceful.

'Just complete and forward the form. Now you can use your pointless writing hobby to create something useful.'

'I don't understand,' said a confused Agatha.

'You have notepaper and writing materials—yes?' Agatha agreed. 'Mother's a snob and demands a butler with impeccable credentials.' He stopped and looked at her. 'You're not taking notes.'

She took a deep breath then headed to her writing desk muttering en route. 'This is unfair and cruel; in fact you're being a bully, Archie.'

He ignored her and kept up the bossy boots routine. 'That'll teach you to be a plain, plump, frump reporter. Now write!' Agatha shook her head but did as commanded. 'Hire an upper-crust butler. Next. Elvira needs an escort for her society debut. Find a polo-playing prince. Contact my old chum Captain Arthur Eastbourne in London. I think his secretary is Miss Orange. Arthur will know the eligible young men around town and send the right chap.'

'Your secretary should be doing this,' she protested.

'I don't want my dirty linen washed in public, and this way, you can actually contribute to the health and wealth of my family.' Not *our* family, mind, but *my* family.

She finished taking notes in preparation for the letter writing. 'And will that be all, *master*?' she asked with undisguised sarcasm.

'Next, contact my solicitor. I wish to change my will.'

'Do you think that's wise?'

'Damn you, Agatha. It's none of your business but if you must know, I plan to keep Elvira quiet by cashing in my insurance policy of ten thousand pounds. She's a loose cannon and could damage, or more likely, seriously damage my business.'

'But ten thousand is a small fortune!'

'And finally, Agatha, you will never write again. Agatha Crispie is now Mrs Archibald Walloman, wife, daughter-in-law and stepmother, and your murder mystery writing days are dead and buried. Do I make myself clear?'

'Perfectly.' She wanted to cry but refused to give him the pleasure.

He rubbed salt into her wound. 'By pursuing your risible hobby, you have become a laughing-stock and a threat to the outstanding reputation of the Walloman name.'

She fought back. 'How absurd. You're angry because I made a fool of you with my disguise.'

She spoke the truth but he would never agree. He tried bluffing his way through. 'You will attend to those letters and the matter with my solicitor, and then supervise the purchase and installation of new curtains in the dining-room.' He spoke the next sentence with as much sarcasm as he could muster. 'And in case you've forgotten, the dining room is down the corridor, that way!' He made eye contact and pointed. 'Remember?'

'Sarcasm doesn't suit you, Archibald.'

'I intend giving dinner-parties which you will oversee and attend. Do I make myself clear?' She paused. 'Well?' She gave the smallest of nods. Satisfied and feeling his dominant position secure at last, he headed for the door. 'The mysteries are no more, Agatha. The writing is dead!' He turned at the door. 'Final chapter. The end,' he said, then left and closed the door.

It was easy for Agatha to cry. She returned to the settee, put her face in her hands and sobbed quietly. She had thought long and hard before accepting Archie's marriage proposal. She wanted security, companionship, and the chance to fulfil her dream of becoming a writer of murder mysteries.

Her unhappy first marriage raised its ugly head. It ended in acrimony and divorce and now it seemed her current marriage would go the way of the first. Her best friend, Bea, wanted to warn Agatha about Archie and it appeared that Bea, spinster of this parish, knew far more about men than the twice-married Agatha.

In the library, the only sound was Agatha crying. She stopped when a soft door knocking was heard, quickly repaired her face, and sat back trying to look relaxed as Pimms appeared.

'Is everything all right, Madam?'

'Yes, thank you, Pimms, everything is fine.'

Pimms approached. 'If you don't mind me saying so, Madam, you don't look fine.'

Agatha sniffed. 'Tell me, Pimms, have you ever been married?'

She sat beside Agatha. 'Nah, I never could see the sense in it.' She felt her chin. 'Anyway, I've got me *own* whiskers.' Agatha smiled—a little. 'I don't suppose you'd care for a sherry, Madam?'

Agatha looked at Pimms, stood and headed for the bookshelf. 'Not sherry, Pimms, let's have something stronger.' She began searching for the book behind which was hidden a wee tot of single malt. Pimms looked surprised. Agatha had trouble. 'It's here I'm sure.' She struck gold. 'Ah, found it.' She removed the flask and examined it. 'Strange. I seem to remember more here the last time I looked.'

Pimms looked into the garden. 'It could be the evaporation, Madam. We've had a spell of warm weather this month.'

'We have indeed. Now, glasses, Pimms; this calls for a celebration.'

Pimms fetched the glasses and Agatha poured a wee amount in each glass. Pimms looked at the levels, particularly in her glass, and Agatha understood. A toddy top-up ensued.

'And just what are we celebrating, Madam?'

'We are celebrating my wonderful husband, his super-friendly family and our glorious future.'

'Celebrating any of the Wallomans doesn't appeal to me, Madam. Did I miss something these past few months?'

'Forget them because I have news. I've been given a new life, Pimms. I'd like you to meet your boss, Missus Boring Housewife.'

'You boring, Madam? Never.'

Agatha raised her glass. 'A toast, Pimms.'

Pimms raised her glass. 'To your glorious future, Madam.'

'To us, Pimms.' They clinked glasses and sipped. 'To new curtains and flower-arranging and to the Mistress of the Manor.'

Pimms joined the toast. 'To the manner of the mistress, Madam.'

Agatha drained her glass, handed it to Pimms and sat on the settee. Pimms returned the glasses and flask to their respective places. She watched her mistress from behind. Pimms knew trouble was brewing in this library, this house and this marriage.

Agatha spoke to Pimms but neither made eye contact. 'Time to be honest, Pimms.' She paused. 'I'm afraid it's all over.'

Pimms misunderstood. 'Don't say that, Madam. Every married couple has their ups and downs.'

Agatha didn't hear her maid. 'My writing career is no more.'

Pimms now understood and changed tactics. 'No, don't give up, Madam. You've still got lots of good ideas.'

'It's not a lack of ideas, Pimms. It's the quality of said ideas, my ability to plot and write, and finally, my husband and his family.'

Pimms swore under her breath. 'Sod 'em,' she murmured which Agatha didn't hear being lost in her misery.

'It can be nigh on impossible convincing an agent or publisher your work is good but I can't even convince my own family.'

Pimms came and sat beside Agatha. 'You've convinced me, Madam, and I'm better than family; much better.'

Agatha heard the comment and looked at Pimms. They both smiled, and Agatha squeezed Pimms' arm.

'Thank you,' she said. 'But I'm afraid the world will never have the opportunity to read my mysteries such as *Evil under the Moon* or *Murder on the Oriental Express*.'

'What a shame, Madam. I like them names.'

'No-one will ever enjoy *The Witness for The Defence* or my favourite, *The Rat Trap*.'

'Must you stop writing, Madam? I mean, why let your horrible family win?'

Agatha thought aloud. She questioned her own ability. 'Maybe it's because they're right. Maybe it's because I have little or no talent.'

A pause, rich with embarrassment, took over and Pimms didn't know what to say. Agatha chose to come clean.

'Pimms, you've served my family forever.'

'I think even longer, Madam.'

'Well now I need your help.'

'Certainly, Madam, anything you ask.'

'I want you to destroy every scrap of paper I possess.'

Pimms didn't anticipate such an instruction and Agatha's request genuinely shocked the maid. 'Destroy your writing!?'

Agatha nodded. 'Everything.'

Pimms was upset. She didn't want to disobey but had serious problems following that order. 'No, Madam, I can't do that!'

'You can and you will.'

'No!'

'And you will never, ever repeat this conversation.' Agatha paused. 'Pimms?'

Pimms was in shock, distraught even. 'Oh Madam, why?'

Agatha could not control her emotions. 'I fear this may be the end, Pimms. My life is ruined but I do not want you to suffer.'

Distress levels for the maid kept rising. 'Oh Madam, stop! Please don't talk like this.'

Both had tears in their eyes. 'I'm afraid, Pimms, you may never work for me again.'

'You can't mean that, Madam. Think of your mother and your grandmother. What would those lovely ladies think if they saw you now and heard what you're saying?'

Agatha struggled. She pushed Pimms' question aside. Losing her dream, her passion to write was the knockout punch.

'Sometimes life is too hard, Pimms. When you can't pursue the thing you love, the desire to go on living, it just fades away.'

The marker on the emotion scale moved up a notch or two and Pimms thought Agatha was losing her grip on life, her will to live.

'Madam? You mustn't think those thoughts or say those things.'

'And whatever happens next must forever remain a secret.'

Agatha looked at Pimms and spoke with her eyes. Pimms conceded and nodded. 'You have my word, Madam.'

Agatha nodded her thanks. Their conversation, their final conversation was over. 'Thank you. Now, Pimms, I'd rather be alone.'

Pimms paused but proved obedient until the end. 'Very good, Madam,' she said, stood and walked slowly to the door where she stopped. 'Madam?'

'I'm still here, Pimms.'

'I've really enjoyed being your maid, Madam.'

Agatha spoke through her tears. 'Thank you, Pimms.'

'And I'd be especially upset if you was to do anything silly.'

Agatha smiled. 'I'm fine, Pimms, thank you; really, I'm fine.'

'You don't *look* fine, Madam.'

Agatha nodded. 'I'm okay. Now, off you go.'

'And I never did know it was you dressed up as that reporter.'

Agatha was pathetically pleased. The genuine compliment was appreciated but came as too little too late. 'How kind you are.'

Pimms paused. 'Goodbye, Madam.'

Agatha paused. 'Goodbye, Pimms.'

The maid didn't dawdle. She took off as fast as her elderly body allowed, closed the library door and fled to her room. Agatha wiped her eyes then went and sat at her desk. She spoke aloud.

'And now for the final chapter,' she said and resumed writing the mystery she had worked on earlier when interrupted by Lavinia.

'Poisons. ... arsenic, cyanide ... ah, warfarin provides a rapid and painless death.' She put down her pen and thought aloud. 'It would be perfect for my final scene.' Her mind buzzed with ideas as she wrote. 'O death, where is thy sting? O grave, where is thy victory?' She wrote and spoke emphatically. 'The end!'

She placed her pen on her desk, straightened the pages, and made adjustments making sure everything was left neat and tidy.

She walked to the bookcase, removed the flask of whisky, clutched it to her chest and began to uncontrollably weep. She took a large swig then replaced the flask because a thought sent her back to her desk where she wrote.

Dearest Bea
I hope you are well. I'm not. I'm thinking of
you as I write. You are my best friend and I
could not have wished for anyone better.
Stay well my darling girl.
All my love.
Aggie
xoxox

Chapter 16

IT WAS NEARLY A WEEK since the fiasco in the library. Miss Mary Mead and Scotland Yard's finest, not-quite-right and thankfully retired Inspector Dithering investigated the case of the body in the library. But being a pretend murder, nothing needed investigating. The family delighted in pouring scorn upon Agatha and her laughable, unpublished plot.

Within the Walloman house, she became persona non grata. They loved to hate her and Pimms, being part of the Agatha package, was detested even more.

The Walloman women sat in their main sitting room. It was big. All of Miss Mary Mead's cottage would fit inside the Walloman main sitting room—easily. Even the Walloman snug was roomy enough for a small knees-up.

A magnificent inglenook dominated this huge sitting room. You could stand up inside either side of the impressive grate. Logs were stacked on both sides, with the fireplace tongs standing to attention as if on guard. Cleaning the grate and setting the fire took an age. Pimms had been assigned the job on many occasions. You could say she knew the inside of the fireplace better than the labels on the Walloman whisky bottles.

Elvira continued to fret over the gentleman, as yet unknown, who would escort her to Countess Kossaroff's social event of the year. It was the launching pad for Buck House and more besides. Archie had promised his darling daughter—otherwise known as the obnoxious offspring—he would find and deliver an upstanding young aristocrat to be her partner. Promises, promises.

Lavinia had equally demanded a new line-up of servants including a butler with impeccable credentials. More promises from Archie.

Elvira recently acquired expensive drop ear-rings and was giving them a spin around the family; well, to her gran. Elvira turned her head from side to side so her grandmother could admire them. Lavinia was not getting a close up. The couple were hardly sitting on top of one another as the furniture matched the size of the room. You didn't have to shout to be heard but it helped.

Back in the library, Archie examined his wife's writing desk. He couldn't find whatever it was he sought, and grew increasingly frustrated and annoyed.

He stormed into the sitting room and began his rant. His mother and daughter were used to these flights of fury and ignored him.

'Nothing!' he cried. 'No notes, letters or manuscripts.' His outrage was wasted on his family. He leant against the solid door hoping to attract their attention. He failed.

'Archibald, what news of my new butler? You promised me a quality domestic last week,' said Lavinia growing impatient.

'And who is my escort to the ball, Father? You promised me the gentleman's name and identity last week,' said Elvira, threatening.

Archie stamped his foot and shouted. 'Damn!' The women exchanged glances. He approached, cursing. 'Damn, damn, damn!'

'Behave, Archibald,' demanded his mother.

'How dare you use such language with ladies present,' snapped his daughter.

He tried to explain. 'She didn't make copies of those letters.'

'What letters? What are you talking about?' asked Lavinia.

'Your new butler and boyfriend,' he replied grabbing their attention. 'I asked Agatha to write letters to arrange the matters I promised, and now I can't find copies of those letters.'

'Are you sure she actually wrote them?' asked Lavinia.

'Can she actually write?' asked Elvira.

'She did and I signed them. My instructions were crystal clear. Shift Simms, hire a butler, and arrange Elvira's escort—explicit instructions.'

'And you were to stop her writing those ridiculous murder mysteries,' said Lavinia.

'Oh that was the first instruction,' added Archie, still fuming.

'Well send for her Archibald and make her explain,' said Lavinia with a flick of her hand.

Now on that matter, Archie was in strife. You see the head of the household had a secret and hated having to reveal same. It made him look weak—make that weaker. He spoke in barely a whisper. 'I can't,' he said.

Elvira scoffed at her absent stepmother. 'She's been sulking in her room for days. Talk about being childish and a sore loser.'

'You should never have married the woman,' snapped Lavinia, and her remark boosted Archie's anger. He snapped.

'Mother! Will you please stop saying that?' Being single was a major social pain for Archie. Being a divorcee would be even worse.

Elvira wanted to know. 'Well, where is the woman?'

Archie flopped back into his soft replies. 'She's left me.'

Elvira thought of a joke, the first in her lifetime. 'You haven't murdered her by any chance?' She laughed at her own self-awarded witticism and her grandmother joined in by snorting.

'Oh yes, you haven't done her in have you? I thought the paving stones looked a little out of place yesterday. Did you bury her well?'

This provoked even more mirth between the females not shared by the frustrated Archie. He repeated his soft voice news. 'She's left me.'

Elvira and Lavinia continued their mocking game. 'I know,' said the stepdaughter, 'she's thrown a tantrum.' Elvira launched into a bout of exaggerated crying. 'Oh boo-hoo-hoo, nobody likes my stories. I'm an unpublished and unwanted failure.' More fake tears.

Lavinia was fed up and turned on her son. 'Tell your wife to stop snivelling, to grow up and follow your orders.'

Archie increased his volume level. 'I can't.'

Lavinia went even louder. 'Can't? What do you mean, can't? You're the husband. Make her!'

It was the trigger for Archie. He didn't try to hide the truth a moment longer. He roared. 'I can't make her do anything because she's gone!'

116

Shock smacked both women who spoke as one. 'Gone!?'

'Gone where?' demanded Elvira.

Lavinia wanted specific details. 'What do you mean? Gone shopping? Gone to church? Gone mad? What?'

'No, gone as in disappeared, as in no longer here, as in she's left me. And to answer your next question, no, I don't know where.'

Lavinia sniffed her contempt for the woman. 'Have you looked?'

'Of course I've looked,' snapped Archie, 'everywhere.'

Elvira smiled and clapped her hands. 'Oh I say. It's not possible she's actually dead?'

Archie had more news and fell back into his nervous and worried state. 'All her manuscripts are gone, her bed is made, her wardrobe is part empty, her suitcase is missing, and this morning, there in the fireplace, I found ...' He struggled to speak. 'Ashes.'

The grin on Elvira's face disappeared. Lavinia blanched. Having her daughter-in-law dead was actually good news but if the dreadful woman snuffed it inside the Walloman home, any publicity from such a demise would be absolutely awful. Forget the stiff. Think of the inconvenience. Elvira rose and walked carefully towards the fireplace. She stayed back for obvious reasons. What she saw made her freeze. She gasped and pointed.

'There *are* ashes in the fireplace!'

Archie feared the worst and even his mother began to believe in the possibility of, dare she even think it, suicide.

'She's killed herself,' said Lavinia. 'The monstrous woman has finally ruined this family.' Not, how terrible was the death for the victim or her family, but how inconsiderate it was for the Wallomans.

Elvira explained what she believed must have happened. 'She has crawled into the grate and done herself in.' Lavinia squirmed.

Archie didn't want to believe it. 'Don't be revolting.'

Elvira pointed at the fireplace and panicked. 'It's her!' She thought of a pun and smirked. 'Look, she's been done to a Crispie.'

Archie ventured forth for another look, a better examination. 'It *can't* be her. There's only a handful of ash.'

Elvira was convinced. 'Fire consumes everything, Father. Those are Agatha's ashes!'

Lavinia's hatred overflowed. 'Not content with excruciating prose, she's deliberately disgraced us by creating an appalling suicide.'

Archie argued. 'Look, we don't know that. And it may not be her.'

'Oh, it's someone else is it?' sarcastically asked Lavinia. 'What, the milkman delivered four pints, wandered into the sitting room, hopped into the inglenook and cooked himself. Or maybe it was the postman or Weeding. Yes, it's him. I haven't seen Weeding for days.'

'Mother, you're overreacting,' snapped an angry Archie.

'Well when did you last see her?' asked Lavinia

'About a week ago! She could be anywhere; even Yorkshire.'

Elvira became excited. 'Oh this is wonderful!'

Archie came close to losing it. 'Elvira!'

Then Lavinia caught the happiness bug. 'Of course; it's the ideal solution.'

Horror filled Archie's heart. 'Mother! Both of you stop this.'

Elvira explained. 'Death, on the quiet, is perfect.'

'On the quiet!' yelled Archie. 'She celebrated Guy Fawkes indoors, in *our* fireplace!'

'So where is she?' asked Elvira. 'Show me the body.'

Archie despaired. 'I can't believe she's in the fireplace.'

His daughter acted tough. 'Well she is and the best news is nobody knows. So copy your late wife and invent something.'

'What?' cried Archie.

Lavinia understood the game and announced her idea. 'I know. She's gone to Canada to research her latest book!'

Elvira expanded the idea. 'To the *frozen wastes* of Canada.'

'Where she met a huge and hungry grizzly bear,' added Lavinia.

The women laughed and kept adding ridiculous endings for the late Agatha Crispie. Archie could stand it no longer.

'Stop it! Stop this outrageous behaviour at once!' he shouted.

His mother shouted back. 'Why? She ruined our lives and besides, her writing's outrageous. No-one will ever miss her.'

Archie pleaded. 'But we can't forget this and conceal her death!'

'We're not,' said Lavinia. 'We'll do nothing now but after a while, when people get used to not seeing her around, we'll report her missing.'

'I agree,' said Elvira. 'We'll report her missing after about twenty-five years.' The women smiled while Archie frowned.

'No,' he said, 'I have to tell the police.'

Elvira screamed. 'No more police! Never, ever call the police!'

Lavinia knew how to win. 'And how will your shareholders react when they hear your wife has cooked herself in the family fireplace?'

Archie put his head in his hands. 'They'll be devastated!'

'Exactly,' said his mother. 'For once, Archibald, start thinking of your family and your fortune.'

His lack of ideas inflamed his desperation. His daughter copied Lavinia. 'Life goes on, Father. Good matchmaking and polite society, the issues which matter, will always be with us.'

'And why should we suffer because of this unfortunate accident?' demanded Lavinia.

'Accident?' gasped Archie, pointing. 'How is that an accident?'

Elvira could take no more. 'Oh please, Father. The woman was unhinged, wrote pathetic prose, was ignored by publishers and when faced with the truth, took the easy way out.'

Archie pointed to the fireplace. 'Easy? It must have been horrible.'

'The woman was deluded, Archibald,' said his mother. 'And the delicious irony of her death is that she finally proved one of her ludicrous plots actually worked.'

'But you can't just light a match and kill yourself,' moaned Archie.

'She was an expert at death,' said Elvira. 'She worked in a hospital pharmacy and clearly knew her poisons.'

Archie hated thinking about it. Lavinia made him feel even worse.

'She put her teeth, glasses, jewellery and unmentionables in the dustbin, doused her clothes in petrol, swallowed the poison, and, just before she passed out, lit the match!'

Archie waved his hands demanding an end. 'Stop, stop, stop!' He paused. 'Yes, all right, I get the picture!' He had never read even one of her mysteries. 'Did she ever put grisly bits in her stories?'

Elvira scoffed. 'Who knows?

Lavinia scoffed. 'Who cares?'

Archie scrunched his face like a little boy lost. 'This is the worst day of my life.' He fought hard not to cry.

Lavinia took control. It was time to play hard ball. 'Now get your facts right, Archibald,' she said. 'Your dear, departed spouse is alive and well, and writing her heart out in Canada.'

Archie collapsed in a chair. His life was spinning out of control. 'I don't think I can face this.'

The women gave him hell; first his mother. 'You can and you will, Archibald. Remember what happened when you were six and came home with messy hair, a missing handkerchief and mud on your shoes?'

Archie looked at his mother and her expression now was the same as all those years ago—fury. She was serious. He copped it then and was about to cop it now.

'You must follow the plan, Father,' glared Elvira, 'or else.'

He shook his head. *What choice do I have?* Reluctantly he agreed. 'All right, all right,' he whimpered, 'Agatha's gone to China.'

The women shouted as one. 'Canada!'

Archie shouted even louder. 'Canada! Canada!'

'For pity's sake, get it right,' snapped his daughter.

'And clear up that mess,' snapped Lavinia, pointing to the grate.

'Yes, yes, I'll have Pimms remove the ashes.'

Both women recoiled at the mention of the maid's name. Lavinia was disgusted. 'Oh she's not *still* here? You promised to sack her.'

Archie fought back. 'Look, I've fixed it. She's going to the local asylum today. Ring the bell.'

Lavinia did so summoning the unsuspecting Pimms. 'A mental asylum is too good for that woman.'

'Why not just have her shot?' said Elvira. 'It would be a mercy all round, and cheaper too.'

Archie saw a possible weakness in the plan to say Agatha had gone to Canada. 'Look, until this asylum business goes through, we should go easy on Pimms.' The women objected. 'But she may ask about Agatha.'

Lavinia scoffed. 'She's too drunk to know anything.'

'I bet she doesn't even know Mrs Embarrassment is missing.'

'But even so, we must be careful what we say in front of her,' said Archie.'

Elvira didn't care about Pimms or Agatha or, in fact, anyone other than herself. 'Now Father, what have you done about my escort? I must have a gentleman from a superior family; minor royalty would be acceptable as a starting point and you can work up from there.'

'Thank you, Elvira—first thing's first,' said Archie under pressure.

Before Elvira could continue her selfish pestering, they heard a doorknock.

'The lunatic awaits,' said Lavinia.

Archie tried being tough. 'Leave this to me. I'll do the talking.'

'That's what worries me,' said Lavinia. She and Elvira were ice-cold whereas Archie behaved like his kittens were due any second.

'Come in,' he said with a voice which cracked rather than crackled.

Pimms entered and wandered towards the family. She was well and truly over the lot of them, hated them even, and had no fear at all. 'What is it this time?' she almost demanded, enraging the women.

'Close the door,' said Archie causing Pimms to roll her eyes, return and close the door, a little too hard. You could slice the atmosphere with a blunt knife.

Pimms returned and struck the first punch. 'I know what you're gonna say.' This grabbed the trio's attention. 'And you three are to blame; all of you.'

Lavinia loathed the maid. 'She's evil.'

'She's deranged,' said Elvira.

'Don't speak, you wicked woman,' said Archie with no impact on Pimms at all.

The maid stood defiant. 'You lot gone and done it,' said Pimms.

'Be quiet,' ordered Archie. 'Be quiet or else.'

'There's room for another in the grate,' said Elvira.

Pimms had been building up to this moment and now, given the chance, let rip. 'You lot have been sniping away, talking behind Madam's back ever since we got here, and now it's come to this. Have you no shame?' They were shocked. 'Well?'

Lavinia seethed. 'How dare you!'

Elvira changed her tune, worried and spoke softly. 'Wait! I think she knows about you know who, about what happened.'

'You lot have wanted this for ages,' continued Pimms. 'You're all to blame, every one of you.'

Lavinia wanted action. 'Have her whipped!'

Pimms threatened them. 'I'm gonna tell the world what you lot done to Madam. You'll regret it, all of you.'

Her body language, her eye contact, and choice of words packed a punch. The goal posts shifted. The trio came under pressure. Each reckoned the wretched maid might be capable of causing them embarrassment which, for these snobs, was tantamount to ruin.

'Oh, somebody just shoot her!' said Elvira with venomous intent.

Archie pleaded and tried to negotiate. 'Come now, Pimms. We've done nothing to Madam.'

Pimms fired her challenge and in so doing, shot herself in the foot.

'Okay then, if you're telling the truth, where is she?'

The trio changed their mood again with Archie feeling brighter. He even sounded brighter. 'You mean you don't know?'

'No, I don't. Last time I saw her she was sad and depressed; she talked about giving up her writing, and deaf.'

The trio were hooked and spoke as one. 'Deaf?'

'Yeah, deaf! So what have you done with her, hey? Where is she?'

Pimms demanded so much and with such ferocity the trio, one at a time, felt obliged to answer.

'Trip,' said Lavinia.

'Sick,' said Archie.

'Gone,' said Elvira.

Pimms reckoned, no, *knew* they were lying. Archie recovered first and explained their short answers.

'She's gone on a trip to visit a sick friend in China.'

'Canada' snapped his relatives.

'Canada,' shouted Archie. He hated making the same mistake twice. He would have made a hopeless criminal.

Pimms stared at the Walloman trio. She thought about the explanation then dropped her anger level.

She thought fondly of Agatha. 'Yeah, that even sounds like one of her crazy stories.' Inside she was smiling.

Silence settled in the room. Each side was thinking of their next move. The trio felt better now because Pimms appeared to be as ignorant about Agatha as they were.

Elvira spoke in a delighted whisper. 'She doesn't know. She really doesn't know.'

'And you're sure?' asked Pimms. 'This trip to Canada to see a sick friend, I mean?'

They thought they had her now so the mood switched again with the trio reverting back to hatred and anger.

Lavinia spat her response. 'Do you think we'd stoop to telling lies?'

It was back to insults at ten paces. 'Telling lies?' scoffed Pimms. 'You lot'd stoop to murder!'

The Walloman women were ready to physically attack the elderly domestic. They were sure she deserved it. Archie was more cautious. He saw several issues moving towards a resolution, and wanted no slips twixt cup and lip.

'Now Pimms,' he said. 'I have a job for you. Fetch your dustpan.'

'Say please,' said Pimms refusing to move. Both Lavinia and Elvira developed blood pressure problems. Attacking the maid became a real possibility. Archie couldn't bear to have a real murder in his house so yielded to the domestic's request.

'Please,' he said.

But Pimms wasn't finished. 'All right. But first I've got questions.' She looked them all in the eye then set off. When she reached the door she stopped and spoke. 'And when I come back, I want answers.'

'Leave!' screamed Elvira coming under great stress. The longer the dreaded maid remained, the greater the risk Elvira's high society escort would witness Pimms and her revolting behaviour; a disaster for Elvira. Her entrance into society would be over before it began.

Lavinia could stand it no more and turned on her son. 'I order you to dismiss the woman the moment she returns. Do you hear me, Archibald?'

He heard his mother but was coming round to the belief Pimms really *did* know what happened to Agatha, and where the mystery writer was at this precise moment.

'I think she does know what happened to Agatha,' he said.

'So what?' spat Lavinia. 'No-one'll believe a senile inebriate. I say sack her now.'

'Do it!' agreed Elvira.

Archie felt real pressure. It was most unlike him to speak harshly to his mater but now he snapped back. 'I've told you, Mother. She goes to the asylum today.'

Lavinia was not used to being rebuked by anyone least of all her son. 'Oh, get a grip, Archibald. Show a bit of backbone for once.'

Archie bit back. 'Yes, all right, thank you, Mother. Leave it to me.'

My goodness, trouble stood tall in the massive Walloman sitting room. Family members were at one another's throats. If this pressure ever exploded, collateral damage would be the least of their worries.

Pimms knocked on the door. 'Enter,' called Archie.

Nothing happened as if Pimms was teasing them. *I know a secret* she seemed to be chanting like a child's song. The maid entered carrying a brush and pan. The others sat transfixed. She stood by the fireplace and stared at them. She knew her task but enjoyed heaping pain on these people, the three she so despised.

'Well?' she asked, requiring them to make a statement.

Archie pointed. 'Ah, there … clean the grate.' He looked at Pimms who didn't move. He weakened. 'Please,' he said.

Lavinia and Elvira raged inside, regarding Archie's behaviour as intolerable. He wanted the whole thing over and done with as soon as possible. The women wanted Pimms dead.

She stood her ground. 'Hey! What's going on?' That's the second time you've said "please" today.'

Lavinia spat her comment. 'Get to work, domestic.'

Pimms didn't move and Archie feared a major confrontation was about to erupt. But Pimms didn't snap or make any sarcastic comment. On the contrary she appeared to offer an olive branch. What was going on?

Chapter 17

'I HAVE A REQUEST,' said Pimms, and those four words grabbed the attention of the Wallomans in a vice-like grip. The gentle, bordering on contrite way Pimms spoke added to the fascination of the moment. 'With your permission, I would like to keep some of Madam's ashes?'

The family froze. A chill ran down Archie's spine, the one which, according to his acerbic-tongued mother, he didn't have. The mood turned serious, eerie even with a tangible fear in the room. Surely it was too soon for a ghost?

'What did you say?' asked Archie in disbelief.

Elvira was disgusted. 'You want to keep her ashes? Errgh.'

'I do,' said Pimms. 'They'll be a final reminder for me of Madam.'

The mood swings kept happening. Archie went back to thinking Pimms knew everything about his missing missus.

'My God! She does know!' he murmured in despair.

Pimms appeared calm, seemingly accepting of the tragic demise of her mistress. She simply chatted about Agatha as if nothing out of the ordinary had happened.

'I've known Madam since she were a bub, and I can't believe she would meet such a terrible ending.' The others watched, fascinated. Was this a confession? Pimms became emotional. 'I admit I helped her end it but I was just following orders.'

Lavinia gawped. 'She gave you instructions?' Pimms nodded.

'And you carried them out?' gasped a stunned Elvira. 'You helped her to ... you know, do the business?'

Pimms explained. 'Madam couldn't face living no more. The pain you lot put her through was massive. Most people would crack under such pressure and, although she was a special lady, she cracked.'

Archie felt a nervous breakdown coming on. If this news escaped, his life was over. 'Ohhhh!' he moaned as his legs wobbled.

Elvira struggled to believe the maid. 'Are you honestly saying you helped my step-mother to ... to terminate her earthly existence?'

Pimms nodded. 'Her exact words were, "Not a trace,". She said it was to be called *The final chapter.*'

Archie saw his business, his career and reputation sliding into oblivion or ignominy or both. His moaning continued. 'I'm done for.'

'I've been thinking,' said Pimms. 'I thought the rose garden would be a good final resting place. Would that be satisfactory to you lot?'

Lavinia slipped into a trance. 'You want to turn the rose garden into a memorial park for that woman?'

'I think it would be nice,' said Pimms. 'I can sprinkle a part of Madam amongst the blooms and, as you all know, she liked roses.'

'I'm not well,' said Archie feeling a pain in his chest. His mother and daughter ignored him. They had issues of their own. It was now every man or woman for him or herself.

Pimms remained calm and waxed eloquent about her plans. 'And maybe we could put in a plaque, a special monument like.'

The trio forgot their ailments and spoke as one. 'No plaque!'

'Absolutely no signage,' snapped Archie, hoping to kill or at least limit the damage of the situation. It was his worst nightmare.

Pimms gave a forced smile and shrugged. 'I think you're right. Her stories weren't exactly well-known.'

'Weren't exactly well-known?' scoffed Lavinia. 'What planet are you living on, you ignorant woman?'

Elvira chimed in with, 'They were totally *un*known.'

Pimms ignored her foes and praised her employer. 'Mind you, she did have good ideas, but now it's all over, we'll never read her latest mystery.' She paused. The others had no interest in talking about Agatha and certainly not about her unpublished prose, and definitely not with the appalling maid.

'Right,' said Pimms, 'I'll be getting on.'

Pimms knelt inside the inglenook and dusted. She did so carefully and reverently. The brush pushed the ashes into the pan. Those that slipped through the grate were solemnly collected. The Wallomans watched, mesmerised, fascinated.

When Pimms started singing the hymn *Abide With Me*, the family went from worried to disgusted and back to worried.

Archie found the tension unbearable. He cracked and went back to being bossy and rude. 'Get a move on.' Pimms stopped singing and looked up at the patriarch. He couldn't help himself and for the third time in a day, possibly in his life, he said "Please". Pimms smiled and resumed brushing and hymn-singing. She seemed a happy old soul.

Lavinia cracked first. 'This is too much.' She stood. 'I will not remain in this room with that thing a moment longer.' The others were not sure if "that thing" referred to what remained of Agatha or Pimms. Had Lavinia said "those things", all would have been clear.

She headed for the door and did her usual routine of making her son do the butler or footman routine. 'Archibald,' she commanded and her son hurried to open the door. 'Elvira,' she called and her granddaughter followed. 'We'll be in the library behaving like the superior class of person we are.'

The women left and Archie was alone with Pimms and what was left of his wife. He watched Pimms with a mixture of horror and intrigue. He wanted his wife's demise to fade into the mists of time in no more than a quarter of an hour with 20 minutes his absolute limit.

Pimms finished and took an age to stand. Old age with its creaking joints were the cause but the occasion helped too. It's not every day you sweep up your employer's remains.

Pimms faced the patriarch. 'I'm right,' she said, 'I'm correct.'

'Correct?' asked Archie. 'About what?'

'You and your family have no interest in your wife. You can't even be bothered to treat her with respect after she has gone to that great publishing house in the sky.'

Archie thought the maid was more poetic than his wife, which wouldn't be difficult. He decided. 'I'm going to join my family. You can dispose of those ...' He couldn't say the word. Pimms could.

'Ashes,' said Pimms.

'Dispose of these ashes in a private and dignified manner,' he said.

'Suit y'self,' she replied and raised the pan with the precious material. 'I'll pop 'em on the roses.'

Archie took off. He now believed in "out of sight, out of mind" and headed for the library in a hurry.

He entered as his mother held court. 'Don't you say a word about those women,' ordered Lavinia, referring to Agatha and Pimms.

'They don't exist,' replied Elvira.

Archie had no choice and joined his family sitting in the library looking out on the garden. He said nowt. What a situation. The family could not, would not discuss the suicide in their home.

Many thoughts buzzed inside their heads. *How can we cover up this fiasco? How can this go undiscovered?*

Their reverie was shattered when the door opened and Pimms entered. No knocking, no request, just here I am so live with it.

Before anyone could complain, Pimms spoke. 'I'm taking a short cut to the rose garden; the one with no plaque.'

If wishing someone dead was a crime, all three Wallomans were in jail already. They watched Pimms and the dustpan she carried.

Did anyone have their ashes transported in such a container? Surely she won't spill any contents here on the Axminster carpet.

Pimms headed towards the French windows with the dustpan and its cargo. You could see the rose garden through those windows and all three family members realised they would be able to watch the ceremony; they had ringside seats for the sprinkling spectacle about to take place.

At the windows, Pimms stopped and turned. 'Oh, please forgive me.' Her words and behaviour worried them. *What does she want now?* 'Being family, you lot must want to scatter her ashes.'

Pimms wandered towards the family. Lavinia was closest and Pimms held out the pan. The look of horror on Lavinia's face left no doubt as to her reaction. She pointed and hissed her reply. 'Get out!'

Pimms didn't want to let the family members regret missing this wonderful opportunity to say goodbye to Agatha. Again Pimms offered the pan. 'It's the thought what counts, Madam.'

Lavinia's twisted, snarling face shouted her response. A "no sale" resulted. Pimms offered the pan to Archie.

'God, no,' he whispered looking equally horrified.

Elvira got in before the offer. 'Leave now!' she snapped.

Pimms understood and walked to the French windows. As she opened them, she paused and spoke aloud. 'You can choose your friends but not your family.' She looked at them, sitting motionless. 'More's the pity.' She left the windows open and headed for the garden, announcing. 'Ashes to ashes, dust to dust.'

With the French windows open, garden sounds drifted inside. Birdsong, the breeze in the trees, even a horse whinnying in a nearby field. Many would consider these soothing sounds, conducive to being relaxed and less stressed. They made no impression whatsoever on the terrified and highly-emotional Wallomans.

Archie brought them back to the subject. He despaired. 'She's teasing us. She's known all along.'

Lavinia attacked him. 'And had you dismissed her when I first told you to, this would never have happened!'

For once, Elvira worried about a person other than herself—a rarity indeed. Such were the bulging veins on her grandmother's neck, Elvira thought the matriarch might do herself a mischief. In fact, both women had stress levels well into the red zone.

'Grandmother, please try and remain calm.'

Archie moved to the French windows for a better look. It was like a motor or railway accident with onlookers being drawn to the crash scene. He was torn. He couldn't bear to watch but then he couldn't bear *not* to watch. He suffered mental and physical torture.

He gasped and cried out. 'She's sprinkling Agatha all over the roses.' Goodness, did Archie have feelings after all? Agatha's demise pricked his conscience or touched a soft spot which previously had remained undiscovered; or possibly not, as his next sentence revealed the truth. He shouted at Pimms. 'Hey! Mind my putting green. Don't spill anything on my putting green!'

He burst into the garden to save his precious golfing domain.

129

Chapter 18

WITH ARCHIE IN THE GARDEN, the Walloman women were free to discuss recent events in private. They had the opportunity to unload on Agatha and Pimms yet again and without restrictions. But why do so? Why discuss boring, unimportant topics? Forget Agatha and Pimms, the nobodies, and chat about what really matters in life.

'I have super news, Grandmother and I cannot wait to show you the material for my new ball gown,' said Elvira.

Lavinia beamed. 'How thrilling,' she said.

'All I need now is for Father to organise my escort.'

Lavinia was genuinely interested in gossip and fashion, and relieved to no longer have to think or care about Agatha or Pimms. 'My dear child; this is what matters; ball gowns, bridegrooms and breeding.'

A now smiling and super relaxed Elvira hopped up and headed to her room. 'I'll fetch the material.' She stopped at the door. 'I'm told I'll be escorted by the most eligible gentleman in England.'

'Bliss,' replied Lavinia finding new reasons to be in love with life and herself. 'I can't wait to see him enter this room.'

Elvira opened the library door and nearly died. There stood Pimms fresh from her burial routine in the garden. 'Oh no!' screeched Elvira.

Lavinia panicked and spun around. 'What's happened?'

'Out of my way, witch,' snapped Elvira who beat a furious exit.

Lavinia turned to see what had happened as Pimms made her entrance. 'Oh for pity's sake, go away. You've buried the nobody and guess who's next? So, what now?'

Pimms let the insults sail on by. *Sticks and stones, you old bag,* she thought. 'You might want to know some gent's arrived from London.'

Lavinia came alive. 'What? Now?'

'That's what I said; do keep up.'

'Oh thank goodness; this is the news I've been expecting. Did you say London?'

Lavinia led with her chin, so Pimms obliged. 'Yes it's that place with Big Ben, Buck House and Baker Street.'

Lavinia choked on her hatred of the domestic. 'You'll regret this insolence, you sanctimonious guttersnipe.'

With nothing to lose, Pimms teased the upper-class widow. 'Go on, I bet you can't even spell them big words.'

Lavinia wanted to throttle Pimms but needed further information. 'What's his business? His name?'

'Didn't say. Only that he got a letter from Mr. Walloman.'

Lavinia's excitement hummed. Finally her requirements were to be met. 'Oh at last, finally; I have my new butler!'

Pimms feigned boredom. 'So do you wanna see him or what?'

'Of course I want to see him. Your replacement is definitely welcome. Be gone you jumentous hag.'

Pimms shuffled away, muttering. 'Here we go; more big words from her with the very big mouth.'

Lavinia was finally being restored to what, for her, was her rightful place in polite society. Her dreadful daughter-in-law had vanished, the snivelling servant was about to be banished and now, a new and prestigious butler had arrived. Life was definitely on the up.

She spoke happily to herself. 'At last, we have quality staff for a quality family.' A light knock on the door sounded. Lavinia drew herself up and spoke as would a would-be monarch. 'Enter.'

A shortish, middle-aged man entered. He seemed to shuffle, and wore a bespoke, tailored three-piece suit, with watch chain and bow-tie, and shoes so polished, in the sunshine dark glasses were in. His moustache was whisker-perfect. He stopped and politely coughed.

Lavinia wanted to inspect him, wanted to delight in a servant with perfect manners and an appearance reflecting the class of his employer. 'Ah, come in, my good man. Come in.'

The man bowed and spoke with a strong French accent. 'Bonjour, Madame. Permit me to introduce, 'ercule Grey-Cells.'

Lavinia recoiled in shock. 'You're not English!'

'Oui, Madame,' he nodded.

'You're French.'

Grey-Cells gave a whisper of a smile. 'Non. Not so, Madame. I am from Belgium. But 'ave no fear. I 'ave lived in zis green and pleasant land for many years.'

Lavinia had reservations. There is no way there could be another domestic disaster such as with the wretch, Pimms. 'Come closer.' Grey-Cells took two small steps; his natural gait. He understood the meaning and practice of personal space long before invading same became a subject in etiquette classes. She gave him the twice-over. 'You appear to take a little pride in your appearance.'

'Oui, Madame. I am, 'ow you say, most peculiar.'

'Peculiar? We've just got rid of one of those.'

'Non, pardon, Madame. Grey-Cells, 'e means particular.'

Lavinia felt her doubts ease a little although she wondered about his practice of talking about himself in the third person. 'And you have received a letter from my son, Mr Archibald Walloman?'

'Oui, Madame. Za letter it was addressed to my friend and associate Captain Arthur Eastbourne who is presently abroad in Peru. 'E 'as asked if I would represent 'im in zis matter.'

Lavinia kept probing for any weakness in the new employee. 'We only employ those who have worked for people of wealth and position; the right sort of people. I'm sure you understand.'

The man gave the smallest of nods. 'Grey-Cells, 'e 'as worked for, 'ow you say, many notable people.'

'Such as?'

He was unsure. 'Madame wishes for Grey-Cells to name names?'

'Of course. If they are the right people, I will know them and verify your so-called claims. If they are of a lower class, even upper middle class, your services will not be required. Do I make myself clear?'

The man had met many people of different classes but Lavinia Walloman was a first. Her snobbery was worn as a badge of honour.

'As Madame wishes,' he said, and began to list his former clients. As he did so, Lavinia grew more and more impressed.

'Grey-Cells 'e 'as worked for Count and Countess Andrenyi, Lady Lucy Angkatell, Sir Charles Cartwright, Sir Carmichael Clarice, Princess Dragomiroff, Lord and Lady Edgeware, Sir Bartholomew Strange, Lady Westholme, Lady Bess Sedgewick ...'

Lavinia interrupted being surprised at the last name. 'Lady Bess Sedgewick you say? What a coincidence. I understand a neighbour of ours, Miss Mary Mead, has made Lady Sedgewick's acquaintance.'

The man remembered and hid his annoyance. 'Pardon, Madame. Lady Sedgewick does indeed belong to Miss Mary Mead. There are so many, it is easy to get za little grey cells to become confused.'

Lavinia paused and tried to look unimpressed when in fact she thought the man standing in front of her was ideal. His appearance was immaculate, his list of previous clients was close to perfection, and, despite not being English, he seemed suitably obsequious, an essential trait of any butler or below stairs employee.

'Well, my good man, your credentials appear satisfactory but there is one requirement one cannot overlook.'

'Madame?'

'Discretion. You must exercise the utmost discretion at all times.'

He gave a small bow. 'But of course, Madame.'

Lavinia had given the new butler her seal of approval. She wouldn't announce the fact of course, not to him anyway, it would be beneath her. She stood. 'Now I wish to inspect the roses.'

She indicated the French windows. He did the gentlemanly or butlery thing and opened them for her.

'Ah, ze English roses; What a lovely thing is the rose,' he said. He smiled and bowed. She gave away nothing of her thoughts and spoke as she wafted past him.

'I suggest you become familiar with the house and await further instructions from Mr. Walloman.'

He spoke as he closed the windows. 'Merci, Madame, merci.'

Chapter 19

THE GENT FROM LONDON stood alone in the library. He'd received a somewhat vague message via telegram from his friend Captain Arthur Eastbourne who was at present in South America. One rumour had it the good Captain was pursuing a woman with a view to marriage.

Archie wrote to Eastbourne wanting help in finding a dashing and eligible chap to escort his darling daughter to the Countess Kossaroff shindig. Being overseas, Eastbourne asked his colleague, Monsieur Grey-Cells, to visit Mr Walloman and sort out his problem. Details were sketchy, a characteristic of Eastbourne's, and when Grey-Cells arrived in Devonshire he was none the wiser as to the precise nature of the task.

Lavinia, assuming he was the new butler, verified his bona fides. So while waiting for the case to be explained in detail, Grey-Cells inspected the library. He studied the books and spied one which caught his attention.

'Ah, Monsieur Darwin,' he said removing the text. He browsed the pages then went to replace it when something caught his eye. He discovered that well-used flask.

He withdrew same, removed the cork, sniffed the contents, and replaced the flask and book. He was about to continue exploring when he spotted something unusual. An observant chap was Monsieur Grey-Cells. He inspected more closely and there, between a book and one side of the bookcase, was what looked like a button or lever. If the last book on the shelf had been drawn forward a short distance it would have covered this mysterious object, thing.

He wondered what it could be. He looked around. He was alone. Carefully, he pushed the button and voilà, a part of the bookcase opened inwards—the Walloman secret door.

Grey-Cells was intrigued but worried. He was a guest in this house and had not yet been asked to undertake any particular task. Nevertheless, he tip-toed quietly into the space via the secret door and disappeared. A few seconds elapsed when the visitor exited in a hurry, looking shocked. 'Mon dieu,' he said and quickly hit the button to close the hidden door. 'What is zis thing I 'ave discovered?'

He removed a handkerchief to pat his forehead and moved towards the fireplace, as far from the secret door as possible. He recovered and began admiring a painting, the one the reporter Miss Layers once noted. Without warning, the library door flew open and Elvira entered waving a letter. She sparkled. She was so overjoyed with the news in her letter, she didn't realise her grandmother had departed and a complete stranger, and a man to boot, had entered.

She stood in the middle of the library and read aloud from her newly-arrived letter. 'The gentleman we recommend has numerous contacts with the aristocracy.'

She stopped reading to see her grandmother's reaction. No grandmother. Lavinia had ventured into the garden to check the roses or rather the ashes which had recently been buried therein.

'Oh,' said Elvira, disappointed she lacked an audience for her brilliant news. Grey-Cells coughed lightly. He was good at the gentle throat clearing. She turned and froze. 'Who are you?' she demanded.

Grey-Cells gave his customary bow. 'Bonjour, Mademoiselle.'

Elvira switched to her panic mode. 'What are you doing in my house? Are you investigating anything? You're not from the police?'

'No, Mademoiselle. I am 'ercule Grey-Cells and Monsieur Walloman wrote to my colleague Captain Arthur Eastbourne and ...'

Relief flooded Elvira's body. Now she knew the identity of the man. 'Oh, you're the new butler.'

Grey-Cells could not have been more surprised. 'Butler, Mademoiselle? I assure you Grey-Cells 'e is definitely not the ...'

Elvira needed him sorted. 'Does Father know you're here?'

'Ah, so far Grey-Cells 'as met za maid and Madame Walloman.'

'Oh, well if Grandmother approves, you must be all right. Look I've received a letter with the most wonderful news.'

'Congratulations, Mademoiselle.'

'And I need to have it announced in *The Times* and *The Telegraph*. I want my name, and the fact that I will be escorted to the premiere social event of the season, namely the ball arranged by Countess Kossaroff. Polite society demands to hear my news. Well, the whole world actually. So, how should I go about it?'

'Grey-Cells, 'e would recommend the telegram, Mademoiselle.'

Excited, she took any reasonable advice. 'Then telegram it is.' She fluttered out as if walking on air. Grey-Cells struggled to believe he had come from London to arrange the sending of a telegram to two of Fleet Street's broadsheets. Before he could question the young lady, she read aloud the same part of her letter as she departed.

'The gentleman we recommend has numerous contacts with the aristocracy.' She stopped at the door and gave the "butler" a cursory glance. 'You may continue your work.'

He spoke as he closed the door after her. 'Merci, Mademoiselle.'

Confused and beginning to feel irritated, Grey-Cells thought about leaving when the French windows opened and the patriarch entered. He looked stressed and carried, of all things, a garden trowel. He was in a bad temper having done his best to bury the ashes, the remains of his not-so-dear late wife. His greeting of a complete stranger and unexpected visitor was in keeping with his mood.

'Who the blazes are you?' Then he realised. 'Oh, you're the fellow from London. Mother will be pleased I've done something right.'

Another bow. 'Oui Monsieur. 'ercule Grey-Cells at your service.'

Archie became suspicious. 'You don't sound English.'

'Ah, zat is because Grey-Cells, 'e is from Belgium, Monsieur.'

'Well I don't suppose it matters. But what does matter is my mother's opinion. Have you met Mrs Walloman Senior?'

'Oui, Monsieur.'

'And what did she say?'

'Madame Walloman asked for the names of people I have represented in previous cases.'

'Cases?' Archie was slow on the uptake. 'Oh, you mean suitcases.'

'Ah, I think per'aps there is some confusion, Monsieur.'

Archie wanted answers. 'Did she approve of your previous clients?'

'Oui. Madame was most impressed with the people for whom Grey-Cells has worked.'

Archie was satisfied. 'Well so long as mother approves. Now ...' Archie realised the trowel he held was akin to having a sore thumb. It stuck out. 'Ah, this, yes I've been fixing the roses.'

'*Fixing* Monsieur? They are broken, per'aps?'

Archie answered freely until he realised he might be confessing to a crime. 'Not broken, no. I had to bury, ah, ... dig over something.'

'Grey-Cells too is most experienced at the digging, Monsieur.'

Archie didn't like that comment and gave orders. 'Right, the usual terms of employment but with special attention to Mrs. Walloman.'

'Do you refer to Madame Walloman Senior, Monsieur?'

'Yes, Senior,' he snapped. 'She is the only Mrs Walloman here.'

Grey-Cells wondered if Madame Walloman was the only so-named person here, why was she referred to as "Senior". He was about to press the point but instead referred to the reason for his presence.

'Your letter to Captain Eastbourne was unusual, Monsieur.'

'Nonsense, it was perfectly straightforward. And how is Arthur? Still admiring those flashy cars is he?'

Grey-Cells remained confused. 'Ah, oui.'

Archie wanted action and so held out the trowel. 'Well here's your first task, man. Return this to the garden shed. It's out in the garden.'

Grey-Cells was surprised, even offended, and took the trowel as if it was a thing most unpleasant. He held it gingerly between a thumb and fore finger distressed in case his immaculate leather gloves might attract even a skerrick of dirt.

'But of course, Monsieur. And, please to tell, what is za matter I should investigate?'

Archie didn't understand or like these questions. He wanted a domestic who spoke only when spoken to. 'Investigate? What matter? What are you babbling about, man?' Before either man could speak, Lavinia knocked on the French windows. 'Ah, Mother. Show her in.'

Still making a face about the soiled garden implement in his hand, Grey-Cells shuffled towards the windows. 'Oui, Monsieur.'

'Come to think of it, there is a mystery you can investigate,' said Archie, and Grey-Cells stopped short of the French windows.'

'Monsieur?'

'I'm worried about our mousetrap.'

'Your mousetrap, Monsieur?'

Life was confusing for the visitor. He accepted the case involving a trip to Devonshire as a favour to his friend knowing nothing about the details, and ever since arriving, was asked seemingly useless questions and given most inappropriate tasks. Had these people not heard of the famous private detective, Hercule Grey-Cells? Before he could question the patriarch, Lavinia again rapped on the glass.

'We're not sure the mousetrap will last. So, admit Mrs. Walloman, return the trowel and then sort out our mousetrap mystery.'

Still confused, Grey-Cells bowed. 'Oui, Monsieur.'

Lavinia's impatience shone and yet another glass-knocking episode prompted Grey-Cells to open the French windows and admit the lady. It was tricky as he had a trowel to juggle at the same time.

'What kept you?' snapped Lavinia making her entrance and showing her son how to deal with underlings.

'Pardon, Madame,' said Grey-Cells closing the windows.

Lavinia sat in her favourite chair. 'You've done a good job on the roses, Archibald. There is not a trace of you know who anywhere.'

Archie went into a mild panic, looking aghast. He gestured at Grey-Cells. 'Mother, we have company,' he whispered.

Lavinia looked at Grey-Cells and waved a dismissive hand. 'Oh he's fine; worked with all the right people, don't you know. Has he told you about his top-quality former employers?'

'No,' said Archie not happy with the new man knowing a certain family secret. Grey-Cells stood there observing, wondering what on Earth he'd let himself in for. Archie dismissed him. 'Well cut along, man. Return the trowel and investigate that mousetrap.'

Grey-Cells chose to go with the flow—for now. He bowed. 'Oui, Monsieur.' He nodded to Lavinia. 'Madame,' he said then, juggling the trowel, made his exit closing the French windows.

Chapter 20

'AT LAST, ARCHIBALD, you have done something right,' announced the matriarch.

'Yes, Mother, but he's foreign, and can he be trusted?'

'Did you not hear me? He's worked for all the right people.'

Before Archie could ask any more, Elvira burst in bursting with happiness and smiling like a smug Cheshire cat. Now she was doubly happy because she found an audience with whom she could share her thrilling news. She beamed. 'I've done it. I've sent telegrams to *The Times* and *The Telegraph* announcing that Miss Elvira Walloman, accompanied by her highly-credentialed escort, will soon be making her entrance into the top echelons of London society.'

Archie was more relieved than happy whereas Lavinia was over the moon. 'How absolutely marvellous,' she said and beckoned her granddaughter to come to her. 'Tell me all, my child. Is he a prince, a duke or a viscount? Oh this is so exciting.'

Elvira sat beside her grandmother, bubbled and did something unusual—she expressed gratitude. 'Thank you for arranging all this, Father. I'll be in all the right gossip columns and now simply must have my photograph in *Tatler*.'

'*Tatler!*' exclaimed Lavinia holding her head in her hands.

'At last, Father, at long last you've done something right for a change.' God, she was a pain.

Archie smiled but Lavinia frowned. 'But you haven't told us the name, rank or title of your escort, my child. Who is he?'

Elvira scoffed. 'Oh Grandmother, be patient. Why would I trifle with a run of the mill army Captain when I can have the aristocracy?'

Lavinia couldn't believe it. 'The aristocracy! Oh, how absolutely brilliant!'

Even Archie felt excited. 'By jove!' he said. 'How jolly super.' Elvira lapped up the praise and excitement from her family. All three were now living the good life.

Even Lavinia managed a smile. 'Life is finally becoming real, as we deserve it to be. We have a new butler steeped in aristocratic circles, and now, my granddaughter's magnificent society debut.'

Elvira reminded the others of the best news. 'But you have failed to mention the greatest, the most wonderful news.' Her father and grandmother looked puzzled. 'We're rid of the awful Agatha Crispie.'

'Oh yes,' celebrated Lavinia, 'and not forgetting the pathetic Pimms is off to the asylum.'

'Come on, Father. Surely this calls for a celebration.'

'Indeed, indeed,' said Archie getting into the new spirit of the family. 'Let's have champagne. I'll call the new butler.'

Before he could do so, Lavinia countermanded his suggestion. 'No, no, no, let us have the appalling Pimms for the final time. I'd like to see her miserable suffering face once she hears the news.' Lavinia picked up the small bell and summoned the maid. 'Bye, bye witch.'

Elvira rehearsed how she would speak once the maid arrived. She spoke in a terribly posh voice, even by her own over-the-top standards. 'Oh I say, Pimms. Frightfully bad news, old girl; you're off to the asylum.'

The others joined in the joke and Lavinia added her contribution. 'You'll feel right at home, Pimmsy-whimsy. You'll be among friends!'

More laughter erupted. For the first time in ages, the trio were as one in attacking the maid. It was Archie's turn. 'Oh Dim-Pimms, old bean, you'll be the most frightful fruitcake in the whole darn shooting match.'

Archie added histrionics to his spiel. He raised his hands, placed his thumbs against his temples and wiggled his fingers while poking out his tongue, sending the women into shrieks of laughter.

Lavinia went for the jugular. 'You can drink like a fish, Pimmsy. Glug, glug, glug.'

Her ridicule prompted a chorus of glugs. All three pretended to be a fish opening and closing its mouth, and adding a glug between lip movements. 'Glug, glug, glug,' they chorused.

Unbeknown to any of them, Pimms responded to the bell, entered the library and stood watching the three well-bred, upper-class snobs behaving like twits.

Elvira was the first to spot the silent, staring maid. She froze, immediately stopping her tomfoolery and signalled to her grandmother. Lavinia looked then she too froze at the sight of her sworn enemy. Archie alone continued his antics, before noticing the others were silent. He stopped and turned to discover the cause of the family's new behaviour. He ceased mocking and joined his family in being hopelessly embarrassed. Pimms broke the silence enjoying, for a change, the chance to have free rein in doing the mocking.

'Well, well, it's the upper class at play. Must be all that inbreeding.'

The trio fumed. Archie tried to recover. 'We have brilliant news, Pimms and wish to celebrate. Fetch a bottle of suitably chilled champagne.'

Pimms hesitated. No way would she let them off the hook so easily or so soon. 'What 'ave you lot got to celebrate?'

It was easy for Lavinia to return to her old self. 'Hold your tongue, you stinking shrew.'

Elvira took a different line. 'No, no, let her continue. It won't be for long.' She looked at the maid. 'You're on your way out, Pimms. Like scribbler, like skivvy.'

Archie took control. 'Fetch the champagne and be quick about it.'

Pimms stared at them daring them to repeat the order. Their authority was seriously damaged having been caught with their pompous pants down. She shook her head and exited, imitating her superiors. 'Glug, glug, glug.'

With the door closed, Elvira vented her fury. 'I hate that loathsome creature. Hanging's too good for her.'

Lavinia took a different line. 'We've done well, Archibald. Your tiresome wife is out, a new butler is in, Elvira has an aristocratic escort and Pimms is history. Better late than never, I say, but good work, my boy.'

Having his mother say anything complimentary would normally give Archie pleasure but in the back of his mind, he feared something. He didn't know what but reckoned danger lurked in the shadows. Let's face it, digging over your wife's remains in the rose garden doesn't happen every day. He didn't sound convincing.

'I suppose you're right, Mother but it's ...' He stopped because someone knocked on the library door. He looked at the women then called. 'Come in.'

Pimms entered pushing a trolley with glasses and a bottle of bubbly in a champagne bucket. They stared at her. She stopped and stared back. 'What?' she said.

'That was quick,' said Archie.

Pimms put her hands on her hips. 'So I've managed to survive your nit-picking, do something right, and you're *still* complaining.'

'Well there's a first time for everything,' said Archie. 'Now leave!'

'No,' said Elvira, contradicting her father and speaking with a smug voice. 'Let her pour the bubbly; her final duty in this room.'

Lavinia joined the smug society. 'In this house and in this parish.'

Pimms understood the hatred but was unsure about her next task. Archie explained. 'We're celebrating, Pimms. And I've a mind to invite you to join us.'

His mother and daughter found the idea revolting. Elvira was disgusted. 'Father! Are you insane?'

Lavinia growled. 'Over my dead body!'

Pimms seized on Lavinia's remark and made reference to recent events. 'Certainly, Madam; do you prefer here or in the rose garden?'

Great question, Pimms. Archie struggled to keep calm. Something in his water, he didn't know what, screamed *Beware!* 'No, it's a farewell drink, Pimms. Let's have a glass for everyone. Four glasses, and I'll pop the cork.' Archie moved to the ice bucket.

'Okay,' said Pimms, 'but you'd better make it snappy.'

Lavinia assumed Pimms was desperate for the alcohol. She was keen but another reason occupied the maid's mind.

'Typical drunk,' said Lavinia. 'Can't control herself.'

Pimms enjoyed having a secret. She taunted them with her news. 'Well, let's face it, it's rude to keep him waiting.'

With bottle in hand, Archie froze. His nightmare threatened to come true. 'Him? Who's him?' The other women flinched.

'Didn't I tell you?' asked Pimms, knowing full well she hadn't and trying to make their pain even sharper. She loved these moments.

'No you didn't,' snapped Archie. The trio stared at Pimms wondering if she was teasing and about to announce news they did not want to hear. She was.

'There's an important gentleman outside.'

Elvira was the first to lose any fear and instead, rejoice. She knew, or thought she knew who it was. She smirked. 'Oh you mean, the doctor from the asylum.' She sang softly but with evil intent. 'They're coming to take you away, away, they're coming to take you away.'

Pimms wagged at finger at Elvira. 'Oh, it's not a doctor, Missy.' She paused, ramping up the tension. 'He's more like a copper.'

Bang! The word copper—a synonym for the dreaded word police— exploded and all three family members turned green.

'A constable?' croaked Archie.

'Oh no, sir,' replied Pimms with authority. 'An important family like you lot deserves an important rank. Why, he's a Chief Inspector.'

The trio exclaimed as one. 'Chief Inspector!'

Chapter 21

THE CHIEF INSPECTOR waited outside the library. He was on a special mission, could hear muffled voices inside but understood nothing. However, when the massed voices of the Archibald Walloman Mixed Choir sang fortissimo, "Chief Inspector", the officer took his cue and entered.

'Hello, hello, hello,' he beamed surveying the gathering. Not a reciprocal smile in sight; as the family turned to stone. The visitor looked around then settled on Archie. 'Mr. Archibald Walloman?'

The detective wore a cheap suit, his tie was skewwhiff, his thin, non-descript overcoat was undone with his well-worn hat pushed back on his head. His name wasn't Beau Brummel.

Archie fought hard to stop his limbs from shaking. 'Yes, I'm Archibald Walloman.' He hated using his full first name.

The men shook hands. 'How do you do, sir. I'm Chief Inspector Sapp from Scotland Yard.'

Archie was convinced his life was over and struggled to reply. 'Did you say Scotland Yard?'

Sapp doffed his hat to the women. 'How do, ladies?'

They managed the weakest of smiles and the softest of greetings.

Archie continued to babble. 'What can I do for you, Chief Inspector?' The Wallomans held their collective breath.

'Oh do please forgive the intrusion, sir, but the maid here said you'd be happy to see me.'

Lavinia spoke under her breath. 'She would.'

'And when I heard you lot call my name; well, my rank, I thought you all wanted to see me, so here I am.'

144

'And so you are,' said Archie treading water and looking to his family members for help, any help whatsoever. They saw his predicament and mimicked Archie.

'We did call your rank,' said Lavinia, wondering what the family had done to deserve such punishment from Heaven. Sapp believed them all to be sincere with nothing to hide, which pretty much illustrates his level of competence, or lack thereof.

Pimms enjoyed watching the Wallomans squirm and suffer, and plunged the knife ever deeper, by raising the situation with the unopened bottle of champagne. 'So what's doing with the champers?'

Sapp became interested. 'Having a celebration are we, sir? Had some interesting news have we, Mr Walloman?'

Archie's panic spread. 'Oh no, sir, nothing special, nothing at all.'

Lavinia tried to help her son. 'We always take a glass between meals, Chief Inspector. Will you join us?

Mr Plod declined. 'Thank you no, ma'am. I'm on duty.' He wasn't but always claimed to be even when at home in the bath.

Archie took a blow below the belt. 'On duty?' he croaked.

Elvira, like her grandmother, kept calm in the crisis. 'It's a farewell drink,' she said. 'Sadly our maid, Pimms, is about to leave us.'

Archie ran with the theme. 'Yes, indeed.' He nodded to Pimms. 'Jolly sad to see you go, Pimms, old chap.'

She milked the moment for all it was worth. Indignantly she asked, 'What, *before* the champagne?'

Lavinia tried to ease Pimms out of the room. 'They say Torquay is very nice this time of year, especially for retired domestics.'

Elvira tried to help. 'Oh yes, so it is. Okay, Pimms, off you go.'

Pimms added confusion to her indignation. 'What, to Torquay?'

Archie produced a hollow laugh. 'No, no, no; to the kitchen.' He went and opened the door. 'We'll call if we need anything. Cheerio.'

Pimms was beaten. She hesitated then ambled out. Archie closed the door and began praying he could do the same with the detective.

'She's such a wonderful maid is our Pimms,' lied Elvira.

'She's been with us forever,' lied Archie.

'You can't find the staff you know,' lied Lavinia.

A tense pause sat uneasily in the room with the family thinking. *Why is he here? What does he want? And how the hell can we get rid of him—pronto?*

Sapp took the hint. 'Well, I suppose you're all wondering what I'm doing here.' They were and stared at him. He went all coy, and appeared embarrassed. 'This is tricky. It's ah, rather delicate.'

None of the family knew what to say. *What on Earth does rather delicate mean?* Archie went first. 'Not lost are we, sir?'

Sapp laughed, nervously. 'No, no, I'm definitely in the right place.'

Archie probed further. 'Delicate you say? In what way is your visit rather delicate, Detective Inspector?'

'Chief Inspector,' corrected Sapp.

'Of course,' said Archie grinding teeth, 'Detective Chief Inspector.'

Sapp took a deep breath and came straight out with it. 'I'm here, Mr Walloman, because of your wife.'

A new bombshell exploded in the Walloman library. Just when they thought the absent Agatha was dead and buried, figuratively, literally or whatever, up she pops again and by courtesy, of all people, the police.

The women went pale, Archie went paler. 'My wife?' he mumbled.

Sapp explained. 'I've received a letter, sir, which suggests your wife may be ....' He stopped mid-sentence, torturing the family, and appeared reluctant to finish.

Archie, without trying, made a death rattle type sound. 'Ohhhhh.'

The detective looked at Archie and was immediately concerned. He moved to help the host. 'Mr. Walloman! You look terrible, sir. Should we send for a doctor?'

His family believed this police time bomb could explode and ruin their lives forever, and having a doctor arrive would probably make matters worse. Archie knew this. *We must keep this in-house.* He did his family proud and fought to retain a semblance of normality.

'No, no, thank you, I'm fine.'

'Are you sure?' asked Sapp

Lavinia was sure and gave her son a warning barely disguised as a threat. 'You mustn't upset yourself, Archibald. There is nothing wrong.' She spoke with emphasis. 'Do you understand?'

Archibald could read between the lines of his mother's dialogue; even between her looks. He gave a weak nod. 'Yes, I understand.'

Sapp was genuinely concerned. 'I hope my presence hasn't caused any inconvenience.'

Lavinia jumped in. 'Oh no, sir. We love it when an Inspector calls.'

'You mentioned my wife,' said Archie hoping, praying for an innocuous situation.

'Ah yes,' replied Sapp. 'Would it be too much to ask if I might see her?' Oh dear. The trio went rigid.

Archie tried bluffing which sounded more like bumbling. 'See her?' *Does he mean he wants to see her remains?* 'Oh you mean a photograph! Of course.' He pretended to look around the library. 'There must be one here. Let's see.'

'No, sir, I mean in person. Can I have a brief word with your good lady? It'll only take a few minutes, and then I'll be on my way.'

Archie was not much good at thinking on his feet but he tried. He had to. 'Ah, that should be easy to arrange.' He looked worried and his family more so. They had reason to be worried, even terrified. Archie swallowed and took the plunge. He indicated in the direction of his mother and daughter. 'Detective Chief Inspector, may I present my wife.'

Sapp was surprised but you should have seen the women. The detective faced the females both of whom had mouths so open you could have sworn they'd swallowed a fish; a groper not a goldfish.

'I see,' said Sapp who didn't see at all. He stared at them and then turned to Archie and whispered. 'I'm sorry, sir, which one would be your good lady?'

Sapp was the second detective to meet Archie's missus in recent times. The first made a dog's breakfast of the rendezvous, and the second was now odds on to top that first disaster.

Archie tried play-acting. He wasn't much chop but needs must. 'Oh, come now, Chief Inspector; a man of your experience. Surely you can identify my wife.'

Good shot from Archie. The detective was snookered. If he admitted he couldn't pick the wife, he'd reveal himself as incompetent. If he picked the wrong one, he'd look a fool. Mind you, with one woman being young enough to be his daughter, and the other old enough to be his mother, it certainly was a conundrum.

The Walloman wife quiz proved tricky enough when the woman herself was present. It became doubly so with the wife overseas or outside in the rose garden. The detective was in deep doo-doos.

He struggled. 'Oh ... ah ...'

Archie came to his rescue finally enjoying a brief moment of control. But would Walloman win the day? 'Chief Inspector, how cruel of me,' he said, trying to smile. He addressed his family members. 'Come on, darling. Own up.'

This appeared to be a perfectly normal request but left the women walking on eggshells. Had Archie been too clever by half?

Sapp looked from Archie to the women waiting for the "wife" to respond thus saving Sapp from embarrassment. Neither moved. Sapp looked back at Archie wondering why hubby's request was ignored.

It would take a great deal of explaining to detail the thoughts currently racing inside the minds of Lavinia and Elvira. They were in turmoil wondering how to shut down this nonsense as soon as possible, and wanted to know if they could be arrested for thinking what they wanted to do to their male relative.

The matter was solved when, without so much as a sideways glance, both women rose at the same time and spoke as one.

'Yes, darling.' Whilst standing, they died. Solved it wasn't.

Sapp looked at the two frozen, shell-shocked women and at Archie who had caught their frozen, shell-shocked pose. Oops.

The woman sank back into their sitting positions feeling rage and embarrassment in equal measures. Steam seeped from their skulls.

'I see,' said Sapp who didn't see at all. He spoke to Archie in a threatening manner. 'Are you aware, sir, that bigamy is a crime?'

Archie was in more trouble than his family. 'Bigamy?' he gasped.

Lavinia was fed up. 'Oh this is too much. Tell him, Archibald.'

Archie constantly objected to his mother's requests but at least he understood them. This time he objected having no idea why she said what she said or what she meant.

He pleaded, his voice squeaking. 'Tell him!? Tell him what?'

She snapped. 'Tell him the truth.'

Now for the Wallomans, truth was tricky. The truth about Agatha had changed so many times nobody knew which truth was currently in vogue. Archie argued openly with his mother. 'But he's the police.'

Elvira understood and helped her pathetic pater, mind you with anger in her voice. 'Father, tell him about Canada.'

'Canada?' The penny dropped and Archie's relief was palpable. 'Oh Canada,' said Archie. 'Of course, do forgive me, sir; my idea of a little joke. These ladies are indeed members of my family. Allow me to present my mother and my daughter.'

The women give insincere smiles. Sapp did a Queen Victoria and was not amused. 'How do,' said the detective, again.

Archie explained the confusion. 'Unfortunately, Chief Inspector, my wife has popped off to Canada.'

Sapp became less friendly and more suspicious. 'Canada? And you're absolutely sure, sir?'

Archie switched to his offended look. 'Of course I'm sure. A chap ought to know where his wife is, what?'

The deadlock was broken by a knocking on the door. Could it be the new butler?

'Come in,' called Archie, glad for an interruption to the current proceedings.

Pimms entered and Lavinia spoke to her directly if only to deflect attention from the topic of the awful Agatha. 'Ah, Pimms. Have you finished packing?'

The maid ignored the mistress. 'There's a Dr Lavington outside.'

Excitement gripped Archie as his overall plan began to take shape. 'Ah, good show. It's your bus, Pimms. Are you ready to go?'

Pimms was never so relaxed, and kept up her sarcastic replies. 'It ain't no bus; it's more like a prison van from the asylum.'

Sapp had been following the comments but nothing, until now, grabbed his attention. Now it did. 'Prison van!?' He addressed Archie. 'Would this be *another* of your jokes, Mr. Walloman?'

Archie tried to bluff his way out. 'Of course, it's just a way of teasing Pimms who is retiring. But my wife has gone to Canada.'

'No she ain't,' snapped Pimms. 'She didn't go to Canada. She disappeared!'

Everyone recoiled. Sapp because this was new news, and the family because they thought they had conned the copper. The trio stewed. *Oh Pimmsy, what have you gone and done?*

'Disappeared?' asked a now fascinated Sapp. 'Since when?'

Archie went with the serious response. 'Ah, we can't be sure, sir.'

'Yes we can,' said Pimms.

Lavinia fought back. 'She sent us a postcard from Canada.'

'From the frozen wastes of Canada,' added Elvira.

Pimms went for the kill. She pointed and proclaimed. 'They know where she is. Ask them about her ashes.'

The trio died. Sapp came alive. 'Ashes? Agatha's ashes?'

Before Archie collapsed, mentally and physically, he tried for one last joke. 'Oh, Pimms, what a funny little chap you are.'

By now the detective had lost his temper. He came to the house with one simple quest; to have a brief chat with Agatha Crispie. Since arriving he'd been the butt of several so-called jokes, all of which he considered to be in very poor taste. 'If this is yet another one of your jokes, sir, I'm afraid I don't find it amusing.'

Pimms went for the kill. 'They reckon Madam has gone to Canada. But have a look out in the rose-garden.' She pointed. Sapp looked at Pimms and then at the cowering family. He headed for the French windows. 'Go on,' encouraged Pimms. 'Take a good hard look.'

Lavinia made a desperate plea. 'Chief Inspector, this is nonsense. The maid is clearly insane.'

Sapp stopped at the windows as Pimms summed up the case for the prosecution. 'They said I could sprinkle her ashes in the rose garden. I followed their instructions. They know the whole story.'

Sapp sought clarification. 'So the lady's in Canada but her ashes are out in the rose garden. Is that correct?'

It was the smoking gun question, the "when did you stop beating your spouse" question, and none of the Wallomans had any answer let alone even a remotely believable one. Just as it seemed their goose was cooked, they were saved by the bell when a person knocked on the door, and this time it definitely wasn't Pimms.

Chapter 22

ARCHIE FLOUNDERED SO LAVINIA TOOK CONTROL. 'It's Dr Lavington from the asylum. Show him in, Archibald.'

Archibald did as he was told and headed to the library door. Sapp opened the French windows. 'I'll investigate in the garden. But first, I must ask you all to remain in this room until I return.'

He left, closing the windows as Archie opened the library door allowing Grey-Cells to enter.

'Pardon Monsieur but I wish to make ze announcement.'

'Announcement?' asked Archie with all three Wallomans hooked. Was the butler about to announce dinner? Bit early for that.

The "butler" continued. With each case he solved, Grey-Cells gathered everyone together—usually in the library—so as to explain his solution. He was always correct—naturellement. He began. 'I 'ave investigated za mousetrap as you requested, Monsieur. It is in excellent health and Grey-Cells predicts it will last for many years.'

Elvira's hopes crashed. 'That's it? That's the announcement?'

'Oh, and by the way, za gentleman with impeccable credentials 'as just arrived from London.'

Confusion swamped the room. 'But that's you,' said Elvira.

Grey-Cells joined the Club Confusion. 'Pardon Mademoiselle?'

'You're Grandmother's new man while I am waiting for my outstanding escort because some day my Prince will come.'

The Belgian politely sidelined Elvira's comments. 'Per'aps later, Mademoiselle, but first zere is one more mystery to solve. Now zat za family 'as gathered, Grey-Cells will begin.'

Before the famous detective could continue, he was interrupted by a person tapping on the French windows. Everyone looked and good old Pimms made the announcement.

'Oh lovely, it's Miss Mary Mead.' Pimms waved, much to the annoyance of the Wallomans and particularly Lavinia.

Meaning the visitor, Lavinia hissed. 'Ignore her,' she said.

'She's seen us,' groaned Elvira.

Pimms took off for the visitor, acting as if she owned the place, going where she liked, how she liked and speaking loudly.

'Hang on, Miss Mead, I'm coming,' she called. 'Hang on.'

The Wallomans were furious as Pimms appeared to be running the household when she should have been in the van and on her way to the asylum. M. Grey-Cells thought his ears deceived him.

'Miss Mary Mead?' he asked. 'Za *famous* Miss Mary Mead?'

A surprised Archie spoke for the others. 'Why? Do you know her?'

'Oui. All za famous detectives know and respect one other.'

'Famous detectives?' asked Archie in a faltering voice. The Wallomans looked at one another, fear creeping back into their eyes. Elvira experienced a hollow feeling in the pit of her stomach.

'Famous detectives, plural?' asked Lavinia, wondering what on Earth was happening. It was all too hard for Archie.

Pimms opened the French windows and Miss Pimms entered wearing her traditional conventional attire. Locals reckoned she had seven identical outfits with a better hat for Sundays.

Archie put on a front, his smile as fake as his promises. 'Miss Mary Mead, how delightful it is to see you again.'

'Oh, good afternoon. I'm so sorry to barge in but I was passing and saw a rather strange sight.'

The three Wallomans never felt so disinclined to ask a follow-up question. Pimms helped them out—she would.

'Miss Mead, are you referring to the geezer wearing size 12s and digging in the rose garden?'

Oh boy. Pimms just wrote her own death warrant. Right now, any one of the family could cheerfully kill her.

'Why yes,' said Miss Mead taking her cue from Pimms. 'I believe he's a policeman still on active service.'

Strangely this suspicious revelation didn't have the impact it might have done had the digging detective himself been present. Lavinia made light of the revelation.

'Oh him, yes he's our new gardener,' she said figuring the bigger the lie, the better the chance of it being believed.

Archie wanted to cut to the chase. 'How can we help, Miss Mead?'

Attention switched back to the visitor. 'Oh I was thinking about my previous visit when you asked me to solve the tricky situation with the body in the library.'

'What body? You're mistaken,' said Lavinia too quickly.

'We have no mystery. You're misinformed,' said Elvira even more quickly.

'Of course I am,' said Miss Mead, 'but I've discovered a wonderful new mystery which might interest the very talented Agatha Crispie.'

Pimms was quick to respond. 'You're too late. Madam's finished.'

'Oh dear,' said Miss Mead. 'You mean she's no longer writing murder mysteries?'

Archie stepped in to kill the topic. 'Now then, Miss Mead, would you care for tea?'

'Yes, tea,' said Lavinia indicating Grey-Cells. 'This chap can begin his duties as our new butler. What's your name, again?'

The "butler" bowed. 'I am 'ercule Grey-Cells at your service, Madame.'

Miss Mead was stunned. 'Not *the* Monsieur Hercule Grey-Cells?'

'Oui.'

'The famous former Belgian policeman who is the brilliant detective helping the police, and who regularly outwits the sincere but simple Detective Chief Inspector Sapp?'

The Wallomans gave birth to kittens. Pimms developed a grin to expose most of her back teeth.

'Oui, and you are Mademoiselle Mary Mead, the quintessential English spinster constantly solving mysteries and outwitting the slow and often stupid officers from Scotland Yard.'

'Oh, but you are too kind, Monsieur.'

Lavinia finally spoke. 'How can he be a policeman *and* a butler?'

Before anyone could answer, someone knocked on the door, and as Pimms, Grey-Cells and Miss Mead were all in the library, nobody knew who it could be. Elvira hoped it was someone specific.

'It'll be the doctor for Pimms,' she said wanting to kick start the Walloman plan and remove the maid once and for ever. Mind you, with the two visitors declaring their respect for one another in the field of crime detection, an uneasy mood sat defiantly in the room.

Archie manhandled Grey-Cells guiding him towards the door.

'Righto, my man, you can tell Dr Lavington he may have the patient in exactly two minutes.'

Grey-Cells politely protested. 'Oh but Monsieur, I am not ...'

'And bring back the paper-work for the transfer of our dear member of staff.' Grey-Cells disappeared and Archie closed the door. He tried to smile but had fear splashed right across his face. 'We must have everything legal and correct.'

The French windows opened and Chief Inspector Sapp appeared wiping his hands on a handkerchief. Everyone stared at him.

'Well, sir,' he said to Archie, 'there would appear to be ashes in your rose garden but I find it all rather confusing.'

Archie needed a change of subject. 'Ah, Miss Mead, you haven't met Chief Inspector Sapp from Scotland Yard.'

'No, but I'm awfully glad I have. Chief Inspector, my friend, Mrs McCulligiddy, caught the 5.40 from Stuffington last week, and in one of the carriages of a passing train she saw a woman being strangled.'

Sapp was intrigued. 'The 5.40 from Stuffington, you say?'

'We reported the matter to the local police but you might be interested. Of course if it's not true, it would make a marvellous tale for Agatha Crispie.'

The Wallomans died as the police officer came alive. It was as if he'd won the lottery. 'Agatha Crispie?' he said, '*the* Agatha Crispie?'

Miss Mead was full of enthusiasm. 'I think it has the basis of a jolly good mystery, and my friend, Margaret Ford-Ruther thinks it will make a first rate motion picture.'

Sapp rubbed his hands with new-found happiness. 'Oh, this is splendid news. You see, that's why I'm here—to meet Agatha Crispie.'

The Wallomans groaned as one. They were back to the dreaded novelist and this bad situation now took a turn for the worse.

Sapp explained. 'Sir Henry Dithering told me about Agatha Crispie's incredibly complex mysteries, and for years I've been pipped at the post by a private detective, a meticulous Belgian bloke. I thought if Agatha Crispie could give me a few pointers then for once I'd solve a mystery before that foreign chap. I tell you, I live in hope.'

A confident rat-tat-tat sounded on the library door.

The Wallomans did their sums. Agatha Crispie plus Sir Henry Dithering plus this meticulous Belgian bloke plus Chief Inspector What's-his-face all added up to one explosive concoction. No happy ending here, folks. Survival was now their best result. It was time to cut and run.

Pimms broke the silence after the door-knock. 'I'll go,' she said, heading to the door. 'This is getting interesting.'

Sapp kept explaining. 'I'd like to ask Agatha Crispie for practical tips about solving mysteries so for once I can outwit this dapper gent from London called ...'

At that exact moment, the door opened and Grey-Cells entered carrying the legal document Archie asked him to fetch. Chief Inspector Sapp did not break vocal stride, and said the only words he could when confronted by his nemesis.

'... Monsieur Hercule Grey-Cells!'

Grey-Cells reacted with identical surprise and curiosity. 'Chief Inspector Sapp! Bonjour!'

Lavinia lived in hope, more like desperation. 'Chief Inspector, how on Earth could you possibly know my butler?' she asked.

Sapp swiftly changed emotions, became angry and appeared to threaten the Belgian. 'You're too late, Grey-Cells. Agatha Crispie's gone to China.'

Once again the Walloman Choral Society came in on cue. 'Canada.'

Sapp replied, annoyed with his mistake. 'I mean Canada.'

Grey-Cells remained calm and confident. 'I do not think so. But right now, Dr Lavington is most insistent 'is patient should depart. Everything is in readiness.'

155

'Finally, at last, thank goodness,' said Lavinia. She took pleasure in making eye contact with Pimms. 'You, tell the doctor his patient is ready.'

Grey-Cells continued to announce the resolution of the puzzle. 'You say 'is patient, Madame? But 'is patient is not Pimms the maid.'

'What?' demanded Lavinia.

'Za patient, Madame, is you!'

A bolt of lightning landed in the library. Archie and Elvira were staggered. 'No!' blasted Archie.

Lavinia was ropeable. 'Me?'

As instructed by Archie, Grey-Cells had collected the paperwork and held up the document. 'Zis authority 'as been signed by Monsieur Archibald Walloman. It states za patient to be Madame Lavinia Clementine Walloman.'

Chapter 23

THE SHOCKWAVES ROLLED IN with majestic force. They flattened the Wallomans. Lavinia summoned up a single word from the depths of her shallow soul. It was part growl and part executioner's directive. 'Archibald!'

Archie reverted to his childhood when blubbering and excuse-making were de rigeur. 'It's wrong, it's a mistake. There's been a terrible misunderstanding.' He yelled. 'It's not true!'

Pimms hadn't been so happy since Christmas morning in the year 1838. She pointed at the dragon who had tormented her ever since Pimms arrived at the Walloman abode.

'She'll go well in the asylum,' said Pimms winking at Lavinia. Talk about revenge is a dish best served cold. 'They'll love her.'

Archie tried to rescue what looked like a lost cause. He was good at blaming others for his mistakes. 'Grey-Cells; you're a hopeless butler and you can pack your bags too.'

Chief Inspector Sapp was on the case and looked for anything to help him get one over the Belgian. 'I'll take that paper, Grey-Cells.'

Grey-Cells was happy to oblige. 'But of course, Chief Inspector.'

Sapp studied the document and everyone studied Sapp. He became prosecutor, judge and jury. Metaphorically, he placed a piece of black fabric atop his wig ready to announce the sentence of death. 'This would appear to be a legal document signed by a Dr Lavington and a Mr Archibald Walloman,' he declared.

The Wallomans wallowed in a trough of despair.

'Of course it's legal,' argued Archie. 'But it's for Pimms, the maid, not my mother.'

Sapp studied the document again. 'The patient's name is definitely Mrs Lavinia Clementine Walloman.'

The woman in question could take no more. 'This is outrageous. Call the police at once!'

Elvira believed even a whiff of the law would wreck her chances of society stardom. She yelled in a most unladylike manner. 'No, no! Not the rozzers!'

Sapp took offence. 'Just a minute; *I'm* the rozzers.' He corrected himself quickly, 'Police, I mean, *I'm* the police!'

Miss Mead made her first comment. 'Oh dear,' she said and pretty much summed up the Walloman catastrophe. What a mess.

Pimms headed to the door. 'I'll fetch the doctor.'

She barely moved when Archie stepped in. 'Stop!' She did and had to because Archibald, being a flat-track bully, was physically too strong. He pointed at her and spoke with venom. He knew what his original instructions were—exactly. *'You're* the one for the asylum.'

Lavinia lost it. For a senior lady, she defied time and the laws of physics and sprang from her favourite chair. Waving her stick, her fury put the wind up everyone in the room. The words *loose cannon* were emblazed across her chest. 'This is all her doing—*that* woman!' Deep feelings of hatred surrounded her next two words. 'Agatha Crispie!'

Poor young Elvira; she still clung to the hope the stepmother saga would be buried, like the woman herself, and she, Elvira, would rise from the ashes—an unfortunate idiom—and make a stunning entrance into society. She panicked.

'Grandmother! Don't you remember? Agatha's gone to Canada.'

Archie too tried to grasp the straw floating tantalisingly past him. He moved towards the matriarch. 'Mother, remain calm; it's all a mistake.'

Mistake or not, alas it was all over Red Rover, the die being cast. The cat was out of the bag. Lavinia played the role of an old, hysterical woman and played it well, no superbly. She pointed the walking stick at her son.

'Don't you touch me! Don't you come near me! Stay away!'

'Mother,' pleaded, even begged her son.

Lavinia's behaviour was such the authorities would soon be obliged to place her in a strait jacket. How fortunate the appropriate medical staff and equipment were close at hand.

'Put me in an asylum, would you!' she barked at the others and her son in particular. With her stick as a weapon, she jabbed and swiped and whacked at her son. He pulled back and cowered.

He feigned pain even though she made no contact. 'Ow! Mother! That hurt.' His pride was in agony.

Lavinia backed towards the French windows. Being sent to the asylum would be horrendous. But to be so treated when the real victim was the appalling Pimms, drove the miserable matriarch mad.

'Think you can lock me up do you!' she snarled. Everyone was scared, seriously scared.

Archie fell on his knees to plead and to make himself a smaller target. 'Mother, please, it's not you!' Lavinia took one step forward and swung her stick again. It missed Archie but the fear hit hard. 'Ow,' he cried and cringed as would a professional sook.

Lavinia prepared for her asylum entrance exam. She withdrew to the French windows, opened them and auditioned. 'I am not crazy,' screamed the woman who looked and acted like a person who was exactly that. She seemed a perfect fit for such a venue. She grasped the door handle. 'You'll never put me in any asylum!' She pushed the French windows open, stepped into the garden, shouting, 'Never!'

Watched by all, she fled into the garden, giving a remarkable performance, hammy of course but then such a performance was typical of Lavinia—gushing and over-the-top—giving free rein to her vast range of emotions from A to B.

For a moment or three, nobody moved. So dramatic had been Lavinia's performance, it would take a while before the spellbound audience rose to their feet to applaud.

Archie moved first. He hurried to the French windows and called. 'Mother! Come back! Mother!' Then he saw her change direction and his voice changed in tone and volume. 'Oi! Mind my putting green!'

Pimms responded. 'I'll fix her,' she said and opened the library door. She yelled to the doctor and staff who had come to collect her. 'The old bag's gone round the back!'

The three visitors were stunned while Archie and his daughter were enraged. Elvira pointed at Pimms.

'It's *you* they came for—*you!*'

Grey-Cells knew more than the others and explained. 'I sink there 'as been za mix-up. There is a gentleman in the kitchen who 'as a letter asking 'im to be Mademoiselle Walloman's escort.'

Archie and especially Elvira were slapped. 'What?' they gasped.

'In the kitchen?' whispered Elvira. 'Are you saying my prince is in the pantry?' She went so pale, her veins lit up.

'Oh dear,' said Miss Mead which was the softest and most gentle way of saying, "My godfather, what a cock-up!"

Grey-Cells calmly filled in the details, and more pain simply crashed down upon the Wallomans. 'I believe 'is name is Jeeves, and 'e is definitely za butler.'

Elvira had a vision of her own death. 'Jeeves the butler?'

Grey-Cells continued to behave impeccably and provide all the necessary facts. 'Oui mademoiselle. 'e 'as numerous contacts with the aristocracy and ... '

Elvira knew the rest of the sentence and joined Grey-Cells in a duet although she spoke with a flat, monotonous tone.

' ... has recently attended several foreign dignitaries.'

Archie twigged but had trouble believing what had happened. 'You mean Elvira's entry into high society includes an escort who is a butler!?' He looked at his daughter and saw her pain. 'Oh dear god!'

Detective Chief Inspector Sapp had observed the pantomime which took place in the Walloman library over the last few minutes and understood nothing. 'Is there a problem?' he asked being both sincere and genuinely ignorant.

Elvira's face was a portrait of angst. It made Edvard Munch's painting of *The Scream* look like a cheery chappie. She entered the twilight zone becoming part human, part creature from beyond the grave. Her words were clear but her body language put the fear of God into the people around her, especially her father.

'I've been ruined by Agatha Crispie!' bemoaned Elvira. 'She crushed my grandmother and now she's crushed me!'

Miss Mead gave her cryptic response. 'Oh dear,' she murmured.

Archie tried desperately to help his stricken child. 'Elvira, try and stay calm. I'll have Captain Eastbourne find you a proper escort.'

'It's too late,' swooned the would-be debutante. 'It's all over.'

Grey-Cells came alive and looked at Archie. 'Pardon, Monsieur, but did Grey Cells 'ear you say again the name, Captain Eastbourne?'

'Yes, I've known Arthur since before the war.'

'But Captain Eastbourne, told me of your letter, Monsieur.'

'What?'

'e is my friend and colleague. We 'ave worked together on solving many cases over many years.'

Now even Archie's worries were worried. He explained. 'I asked Arthur to help with a certain matter.' As Archie said "certain matter" he indicated his weeping offspring.

Grey-Cells explained. 'Captain Eastbourne, 'e is abroad in South America. Last week 'e sent a telegram asking me to 'elp one of his friends.'

'That's me,' said Archie getting excited. 'I'm Arthur's friend.'

'Eastbourne tells to Grey-Cells, I am to assist with a special case.'

Archie discovered the truth of the debacle, or rather the reason for the mess. 'Yes, to find my daughter a suitable escort.'

Sapp played the role of ace detective to a tee. 'I'm sorry but I don't follow any of this.'

Miss Mead was ahead of the pack—again. 'There seems to be a slight misunderstanding.' What a massive understatement.

Archie had a lightbulb moment. 'Of course. Agatha sent the letters to the wrong people.'

The others wanted more information although Elvira chose a one-way ticket to Oblivion. She rose and began a farewell speech to rival Nellie Melba. She built the hysteria in what many would regard as an outstanding performance with the trouble being she wasn't acting.

'It's in the papers,' she said, speaking at first with a low pitch and volume. Then she began to release the floodgates of death and destruction. 'I'm making my society debut with a butler!' Ahhhhh!' She moved before her last cry had finished. She headed for the library door and fled wailing. 'And it's in the papers! Ahhhh!'

Pimms opened the door allowing the sound of Elvira's despair to linger. Leaving the door open was, for Pimms, her schadenfreude writ large. She delighted in the humiliation of the younger witch.

The action had been fiery and detailed yet despite this, the professional detective, as opposed to the Belgian and the spinster from the village, remained in the county of Clueless. A reasonably intelligent chap would stay quiet and hopefully pick up a clue or two as the events progressed. But no, Sapp opened his mouth and broadcast his lack of intelligence.

'Would somebody please tell me what is going on?'

Everyone ignored the Scotland Yard detective. Archie wandered about as if in a kind of stupor. 'I think I'm going mad. I think I've lost my marbles. What has happened to my life?'

Pimms, still on library door duty, yelled again to the people outside. 'Oi! Hold the van. Here's another one for you!' She directed Archie with gestures. 'This way, guv'nor.'

Under Pimms' control, Archie exited. 'Help! I'm going mad!'

He stumbled through the door, Pimms helping him as best she could. 'Straight ahead, sir; that's the ticket. Like mother, like son.'

His voice could be heard as he headed towards the asylum van. 'Mother! Elvira!' He drew out the next name. 'Agatha! Wait for me.'

His voice faded as did the lives of the three Wallomans.

Sapp came alive. 'Agatha? Did somebody call for Agatha Crispie?'

'They did, Chief Inspector,' said Miss Mead. 'She's the writer of murder mysteries who lives in this house and works in this library at that writing desk.' She pointed, and Sapp looked then came alive.

'Oh lordy lord,' he enthused. 'This is my lucky break. I've found the marvellous writer. She'll tell me her tricky plots and improve my mystery solving, especially ...' He paused, looked and pointed at Grey-Cells. 'Especially against Monsieur Hercule Grey-Cells.'

'You are too kind, Chief Inspector,' said the Belgian, bowing.

Sapp approached Grey-Cells and wagged a finger in his direction. 'At last, finally, at long last, Grey Cells, I've got you. This time, I win.'

He grinned at the Belgian then left the library in search of the mystery writer. His voice could be heard as he searched the house.

'Agatha! Agatha Crispie! Hello?'

Numbers dwindled and Pimms felt she didn't belong with the two detectives. She prepared to leave. 'Well I'd better see to the packing.'

Miss Mead had the ability to ask questions in a seemingly non-sticky-beak kind of a way. 'Does this mean you're leaving, Pimms?' she asked.

'Oh it's not *my* packing, Miss Mead, it's *their* packing. They're the ones what's going.' She left, closed the door then opened it again immediately and poked her head around the corner.

'And help y'self to the bubbly.' She indicated her trolley then left.

Grey-Cells addressed his fellow sleuth. 'A remarkable afternoon, Miss Mary Mead, n'est-ce pas?' He indicated the settee. 'May I?'

She acquiesced. 'Oh, please do.' He sat and she broke the ice. 'I must say, Monsieur Grey-Cells, I've long admired your work.'

He nodded and gave his customary miniature smile. His moustache smiled in agreement. 'Merci, Mademoiselle and 'ow kind you are. Of course, I should return za compliment. Naturally, I 'ave 'eard about your famous "Body in the library" case. Magnifique!'

'Thank you, Monsieur but my humble murders often occur in and around the village. I rarely travel the globe as do you.'

He waved a finger of gentle disapproval. 'Au contraire, dear lady. What about your celebrated stay in Bertram's 'otel in London?'

She gave a wry smile. 'Oh yes but London is much less exotic than Egypt, the French Riviera, the Orient Express or Baghdad.'

Their chat continued with both being polite by nature and adding so much respect for the other and their achievements. Grey-Cells again corrected his "colleague" but with kindness.

'Not Baghdad, dear lady. That case, it was solved by the less well-known, Monsieur Darker Pine.'

'Oh yes,' she said with a smile and leading to her punch line of a joke. 'Indeed, Monsieur. One of the few he was able to solve.'

They both smiled with appropriate nods and gestures.

Grey-Cells turned sad. 'I am most sorry Captain Eastbourne is not 'ere. But zer is so much I can tell 'im when back in London.'

She was surprised and a little disappointed. 'Oh, you're leaving?"

Grey-Cells stood. 'Oui. My secretary Miss Orange 'as sent word of a case I must investigate.'

'But you have yet to outwit Chief Inspector Sapp. Surely you can't allow a plodding policeman to defeat the great Hercule Grey-Cells.'

He nodded. 'Merci, Mademoiselle but I sink not. Za missing Agatha Crispie is certainly not in Canada. I am sure not even in 'arrowgate. I will leave 'er to you and the Chief Inspector Sapp.'

'We agree, Monsieur as I too thought as much.'

Grey-Cells indicated the French windows. 'Grey-Cells, 'e believes the rose garden it is a lot closer, n'est-ce pas?'

'Oh you mean the ashes being the paper and not the person?'

'Oui,' he replied and offered his arm. She stood and leant on him. 'Come, we can discuss za ashes and za hidden door.'

They headed towards the French windows and beyond to the infamous rose garden. 'Miss Crispie has used the hidden door before you know, in another of her mysteries about the body in the library.'

Grey-Cells knew but pretended otherwise. 'She 'as? Please to tell Grey-Cells all about zat mystery.'

He opened the French windows and stepped back so as to allow his fellow sleuth to leave the library.

'I will be happy to do so, Monsieur, if in return, you will help me to better understand the demise of Mr Roger Roydack.'

They entered the garden and headed for the roses. 'Ah, poor fellow, 'e was murdered you know,' said Grey-Cells.'

'I think we both know, Monsieur, I am more interested in the little trick used in the design of the mystery.'

'Little trick, Mademoiselle Mead? Whatever can you mean?'

She smiled and he reciprocated. 'I apologise, Monsieur. I'm sure you agree there are certain secrets we must never reveal.'

He nodded. 'Tell to me, please, would you consider a partnership?'

She smiled, enjoying the idea. 'The Belgian and the Spinster?' she replied.

He smiled. I prefer The Spinster and the Belgian, s'il vous plait.'

They wandered past the roses, past the putting green and kept wandering away from the Walloman estate never to return.

Chapter 24

PIMMS OPENED THE LIBRARY DOOR, happy to be still in a job but worried about her missing mistress. She saw the empty room. 'Oh, all gone.'

She plumped the cushions, tidied the drinks trolley and went to check on the French windows. With her back to the bookshelves and looking out into the garden, naturally she didn't see the secret panel open. Nobody appeared but an eerie voice wafted out from the hidden room. It sounded like Dorothy S. Layers.

'Who raises people from the dead.'

Pimms smiled but didn't turn. She felt happy. It was a voice she wanted to hear. It belonged to a person she wanted to talk to, listen to and share love, friendship and news with; especially news.

Still with her back to the bookshelves, Pimms gave a normal greeting as if nothing had happened in the Walloman house, oh, for simply ages. 'And a very good day to you too, Madam,' she said.

Agatha emerged from her hideaway, her bolt hole. Pimms turned and gasped because the unheard of writer of mystery stories looked different; lovely different, even sensational different.

Agatha whispered. 'Pimms. Is it safe to come out?'

'Blimey, madam! You is dressed up a bit ain't you. Is it a funeral or a wedding you is going to?'

Agatha certainly was dressed up to the nines, wearing a gorgeous grey woollen dress with a striking belt, a stunning hat, a beautiful black coat with a fur collar, new leather gloves, silk stockings and brand new shoes. Cheap would never be used to describe the outfit, and Agatha's hair and makeup topped off the total package. She carried a small and fashionable travel case, and looked like the first-class passenger she planned to become.

'Have you missed me, Pimms? I've certainly missed you,' she said adjusting her gloves and hat.

'Indeed I have, madam although for a while there, I thought you was never coming back.'

'How kind you are. So, has anything important happened?'

'In a way, Madam, yes.'

Pimms hesitated only because she had no idea where to start explaining recent events.

'Well go on,' said Agatha, smiling. 'Don't keep me in suspenders.'

Agatha guided Pimms to the settee where they sat. 'I'd like you to go first, Madam.'

'Pardon?'

'Not to put too fine a point on it, Madam, and excusing my French, but where the hell have you been these last few days and nights?'

'Oh, come now, Pimms. You must know I needed cheering up, and there's nothing like a new outfit or three to boost one's ego. I popped up to Teddington and visited a few shops in Oxford Street to replenish my wardrobe. What do you think?' She indicated her outfit.

'Have you come into money, Madam?'

Agatha laughed. 'My secret savings, Pimms, now, what have I missed?'

Pimms mused. 'What haven't you missed, Madam, while you was in Canada?'

Agatha gasped. 'Canada? Whatever made you think I was over there?'

'Your family for one.'

Agatha was genuinely surprised. 'They thought I went to Canada?'

'Yes but only because I buried you in the rose garden.'

'What?' shrieked Agatha. 'Have you been drinking, Pimms?' They looked at one another and Agatha immediately apologised. 'Oh I beg your pardon, Pimms. But please, you'll have to start at the beginning.'

Pimms explained. 'I will but first I have a confession to make.'

Agatha worried. 'Oh dear, I don't like the sound of that.'

'You asked me to burn all your writing material, Madam.'

Agatha went quiet. She was in the depths of depression when she gave those instructions. She spoke sadly, with a soft voice. 'As soon as I left, I regretted having said that.'

'Well I didn't destroy *all* your papers, Madam.' Agatha lifted her eyes and stared at Pimms. 'I burnt your notes, newspaper clippings and letters but I kept all your stories.'

Agatha looked at Pimms and then they hugged. 'Thank you,' whispered the writer. She pulled back and demanded answers. 'So come on then, what's this business about me going to Canada?'

Pimms explained. She told Agatha everything about how the family thought Agatha had committed suicide in the giant inglenook, and how Pimms allowed them to think the ashes in the grate were human when in fact they were only Agatha's notes.

Agatha laughed a healthy laugh. The more Pimms explained, the greater the laugh. Agatha was thrilled her mysteries were intact and pleased her appalling family had suffered, thinking Agatha was dead.

Pimms worried because the best, or the worst, was yet to come.

If Madam is happy now, how happy will she be when she hears about the fate of the family?

'Oh Pimms, I can't believe they thought I was dead and then made up some lie about me going to write in Canada.'

'All true, Madam, every last word of it.'

'So where is everyone? The place seems deserted.'

Pimms turned serious. 'I have to be honest, madam. You've been a very naughty girl.'

Agatha giggled and squeezed her maid's arm. 'Good, I like being naughty. What have I done this time?'

'Did Mr. Walloman ask you to send a few letters?'

'He did and I did as asked, definitely. Why, what's happened?'

Pimms paused. 'Well I should forget about becoming a secretary, Madam, and stick to writing stories.'

Agatha frowned. 'But I typed and posted the letters myself. Archie signed them. Although I remember, he was in a bit of a hurry.'

'But did you put the right letters in the right envelopes?'

Agatha looked blank. 'Oh dear. Did I make a mess of things?'

'I think mess is probably the right word, Madam. You may not be a successful mystery writer ...'

'Yet,' interrupted Agatha wagging a finger at Pimms.

Pimms finished her comment. 'Yet, Madam but you didn't come down in the last shower.'

Agatha looked offended. 'I'm sure I don't know what you mean.'

Pimms didn't believe her. 'Well I think I was due to go to the asylum but somehow your mother-in-law went in my place.'

Agatha froze and she and Pimms stared at one another. 'Lavinia?' Pimms nodded. 'Lavinia was sent to the asylum?' More nodding from the maid. The laughter began. It was slow and soft at first, more like giggling. Then both women took their lead from the other.

'Oh poor Lavinia,' cried Agatha between laughter. 'It couldn't have happened to a nicer snob.' They laughed again. 'I don't suppose she was very happy?'

'What do you think?' said Pimms. 'And Miss Elvira put a notice in the papers about her society debut.'

Agatha knew what had been requested by Archie. 'Yes, a chum of Archie's was going to find her an escort—a Captain Westbourne.'

'Eastbourne,' corrected Pimms.

'He's the one. I definitely sent his letter.'

'And Mr Walloman had to find a new butler for his mother to replace me when I went off to the asylum.'

Agatha nodded. 'You're correct. I sent a letter for Elvira's Prince Charming, and a letter for Lavinia's upper-crust butler; two letters.'

'But you got it wrong, Madam. The letter for the new escort went to the new butler and vice versa.'

'What?' gasped Agatha.

'So Miss Elvira told the world she had some wonderful partner for the society ball and he turned out to be a butler called Jeeves.'

Agatha gasped. 'And Elvira put that information in the papers?'

'Only *The Times* and *The Telegraph*.'

Agatha laughed with joy helped by Pimms being happy to see her mistress back at home and smiling for the first time in ages.

'*Only!* Oh dear. And what about Archie? I bet he was a little upset.'

'A little upset?' said a disbelieving Pimms. 'Mr Walloman even thought the ashes from your notes and clippings was your remains.'

Agatha's eyes went wide. 'My *human* remains?'

'Yes, Madam.'

'In the inglenook?'

Pimms nodded. 'He convinced his mother and daughter you'd taken poison, climbed into the big grate in the sitting room and set fire to yourself.'

Agatha couldn't believe it. 'No!'

'It's true, madam.'

'I can't believe they'd fall for that.'

Pimms looked a little sheepish. 'I must confess, Madam, I did help them believe, just a little bit. I even performed *Abide With Me* as I collected your ashes.'

Agatha sat back and looked at Pimms. The novelist shook her head in admiration. 'Pimms, you're marvellous. I wish I'd seen their faces.

'Madam, I can assure you they weren't laughing.'

'I'll bet they weren't. So where are they now?'

'Well I suppose Mr Walloman is trying to have his mother released from the asylum, and I think Miss Elvira has joined a nunnery.'

Agatha clapped her hands and laughed. 'Hallelujah!' she cried.

'I think they'll be away for quite a while, Madam; certainly Mr Walloman will be avoiding his mother and daughter like the plague.'

'Well, talk about all's well that ends well, hey Pimms?' Agatha wandered to the French windows to admire the rose garden, her one-time private cemetery. 'I sure did make a mess of things, didn't I?'

'You could say that, Madam. But to be fair, what happened to the Wallomans couldn't have happened to a nicer family.'

Agatha looked back at Pimms who sported a grin. Agatha smiled and then reflected on her recent past. 'I needed to get away, Pimms. I needed time to think about my life and especially about my writing.'

Pimms took a deep breath. 'Do you mean, Madam, you are going to keep writing your murder mysteries?' She crossed her fingers.

Agatha moved back to Pimms and announced her news. 'I mean, Pimms, it's time I took control of my life. It's time for a new chapter. Pimms, I'm off to Australia.'

Pimms opened her mouth. Shocked, she wanted answers. 'Australia, Madam?' But why?' She wanted to ask about her own future. *Will you still need a maid, Madam?*

Agatha opened her swish piece of luggage and checked its contents chatting as she did so. 'Oh you know; change of scenery; a chance to re-charge the batteries before resuming my murder mysteries.'

Pimms was delighted. She stood and clasped her hands together. 'Oh I'm so happy for you, Madam.'

'Now you'll need to hold the fort while I'm gone; scare off the odd stranger.'

Pimms had no idea what Agatha meant. 'Stranger, Madam?'

'They're about. Didn't I tell you?'

'Tell me what, Madam?'

'I encountered this middle-aged gent today. He opened the secret door in the bookcase—how he found the hidden button I'll never know—and there I was trying on my new swimming costume with my face plastered in sun cream. I'm told you need it at Bondi Beach. Anyway, he popped his head around the corner, saw me and nearly had a heart attack.'

Pimms smiled. She knew who it was. 'Serves the sticky-beak right.'

From her suitcase, Agatha produced an envelope and handed it to her maid. 'Now this has my new address Down Under, Pimms, and I want to hear immediately any publisher gets in touch.'

Pimms became excited. 'Oh, are you expecting good news about one of your mysteries, Madam?'

'One is always expecting, Pimms. Writers have a particular genetic disposition which puts them in a state of perpetual expectation.'

'If you say so, Madam.'

'My middle name is Eternal Optimist.'

Pimms thought about that comment. 'That's two names, Madam.'

Agatha pondered then pointed a finger at Pimms. 'Hyphenated,' she said, smiled and picked up her case. 'One day, someone will snap up my stories. Not sure when or which story but hope springs eternal.' She prepared to leave. 'Now for my exit.'

Pimms was embarrassed. 'Ah, Madam.'

Agatha stopped. 'Problem, Pimms?'

'I hate to mention this but I'm a bit short of the readies.'

Agatha felt awful. 'Oh, Pimms, do forgive me, I completely forgot. Mr. Walloman asked me to send a letter to his solicitor. That one I did get right; I hope. Apart from my address Down Under, there's something else inside that envelope. Do please open it.'

Pimms began to shake. She had trouble opening the envelope. Finally she removed the contents and stared at it. The shock showed on her face and she aged in an instant.

'One thousand pounds! Oh Madam, what have you done?'

'It's a postal order made out to you, Pimms, meaning my letter might have the wrong details with Elvira only getting nine grand.'

'But I'm too old to go to jail, Madam.'

'Nonsense,' said Agatha. 'Archie signed all the letters in a rush and it's only a small fraction of what he has stashed away. Serves him right for not reading what he signed. Besides, I'm sure the family would want you to have it.' Agatha winked.

'Madam, I don't know what to say.'

'Say nothing and spend it wisely. And the bungalow in Teddington is yours whenever you need it. I'm off there to collect my suitcase.'

Silence took over. During the pause, both women thought of what they had endured since arriving in the Walloman mansion, and how their lives were about to diverge. They looked at one another and then embraced; warmly and with sadness.

Pimms spoke with her chin resting on Agatha's shoulder. 'Thank you, Madam; you've been very kind and generous to an old woman.'

'Thank *you*, Pimms. You've served three generations of my family and the least I can do is help you enjoy a long and happy retirement.'

Agatha broke free and headed for the French windows. Pimms got there first and opened them. 'Good luck, Madam.'

'Take care,' said Agatha and stepped into the garden.

'Safe journey, Madam and bon voyage,' said Pimms.

Agatha turned to face her maid. 'Now let me know the moment you hear about one of my stories being published.'

'I will, Madam, I promise.'

'Goodbye Pimms.' She waved and walked away. Her carriage was due at the gatekeeper's cottage in fifteen minutes.

Pimms waved. 'Goodbye, Madam. Good luck with your writing.'

The maid kept waving until Agatha disappeared. Pimms closed the French windows and looked again at the postal order made out in her name. She rarely saw her full name in print and wondered how Madam discovered the details. The Payee was *Prudence Isobel Miranda McGillacuddy Smith*. Agatha's grandmother saw her new maid's initials and christened Miss Smith, Pimms.

She popped the document back in the envelope, went to the bookcase to remove her "favourite" book, withdrew the flask and toasted her new success. Then the envelope went in first, followed by the flask with finally the Devil's Chaplin's tome being replaced.

She looked around the empty library, did a sort of swirl, and started to hum *Burlington Bertie*. She was hardly a toff but with the Wallomans running for the hills in glorious defeat, and a thousand nicker in her old kitbag, Pimms reckoned she was the Queen herself.

She sat on the settee then swivelled and put her feet on one end lying back on a cushion on the other. *This is the life.*

The cushion behind her head felt uncomfortable. She wriggled to make the situation better. Having no success, she sat up, lifted the cushion and discovered a newspaper. She dropped it on the floor, adjusted the cushion ready to resume her new lady of leisure position but stopped. A heading in the newspaper caught her eye. She picked up the paper and read.

'Well I never,' she said as the information captured her brain. She read aloud. 'New mystery writer has her first story published.' Bursting with pride, she stood and moved to the French windows. 'Oh Madam, Madam you've finally made it.' She looked to see if Agatha Crispie was still in sight. No, she'd gone.

She continued reading aloud. 'A new mystery writer from the south-west of England has published her first novel.' Pimms shed a tear. 'The world will soon recognise the name of Agatha ...'

Then disappointment hit Pimms hard and her face went from an excited smile to a disgusted frown. 'Oh, and wouldn't you know it? They've spelt her name wrong!'

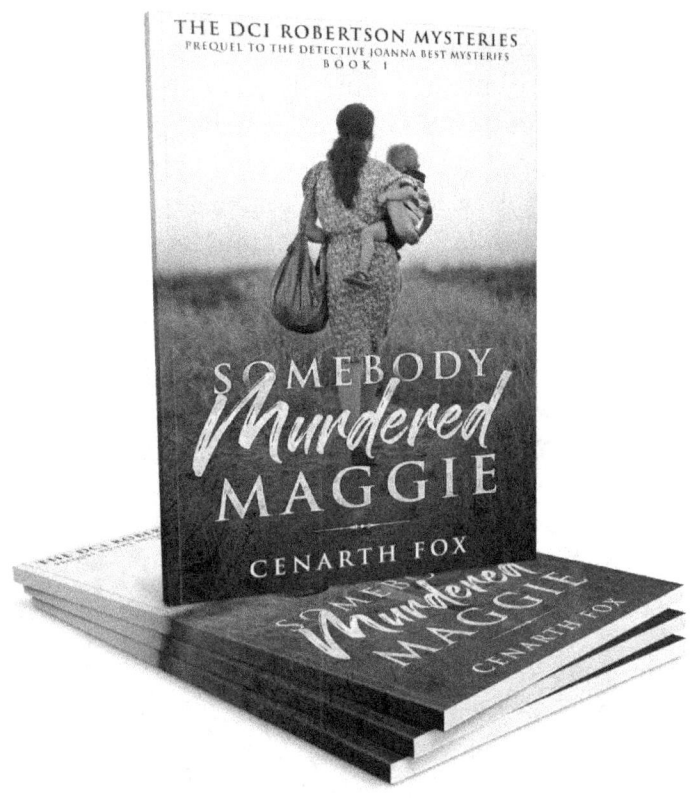

The Detective Joanna Best Mysteries

Jo Best is new to the Homicide Squad at Victoria Police. She's bright, good at solving murders and even better at finding herself in trouble. A few people love her and a few don't. Criminals she meets play rough. Some of her colleagues play rougher. Jo's homicide cases have dead bodies and nasty villains (naturally), a peppering of puns and a solid serve of slapstick. There's even a sprinkling of unresolved sexual tension. Jo gets to travel overseas to Paris in pursuit of justice. If you enjoy police procedurals, crime fiction, female sleuths and murder mysteries, Detective Senior Constable Joanna Best is worth a whirl.

www.cenfoxbooks.com

I could not put this series down. The characters, plots, settings, kept me reading. I really liked the word comedy phrasing. A couple of characters I wanted to smack. **Amazon Review**

Meet the Author

 I always enjoy hearing from readers with their questions and/or comments. I have a regular newsletter (*Foxy's Follies*) with news about my latest books, plays and musicals. It's free. If you'd like to receive a copy, please send an email. I never share the email address of my subscribers.

writer@foxplays.com
cen@cenfoxbooks.com

And if you'd care to post a review of the book on Amazon or Goodreads, I'll be most grateful.

Happy reading

Cenarth Fox

www.cenfoxbooks.com